How could ten years fall away in minutes?

How could a decade be forgotten with the touch of his hand? How could formerly hazy memories of long, passionate nights be suddenly more real to her than the people surrounding them as Gavin took her in his arms?

"A lot has changed in ten years." His warm breath brushed her cheek and she shivered.

Sex, she told herself. That's what this was about. She'd always responded to whatever pheromones Gavin put out. That hadn't changed.

Still, if he was getting ideas that their chance meeting at the cabin could lead to anything more, she needed to set him straight. Sure, they'd gotten along fine, shared an amazing kiss. But that was a kiss goodbye, not the start of something new.

Gavin's hand at th⬚⬚⬚⬚⬚⬚⬚⬚ ⬚ed her closer. She could ha⬚⬚⬚⬚⬚⬚⬚⬚⬚⬚⬚nt she gave herself permission t⬚⬚⬚⬚⬚⬚⬚⬚el of him.

Stop this, Jenny. Stop it before you do something incredibly stupid, said the voice in her head.

Should she listen to it?

* * *

PROPOSALS & PROMISES:
Putting a ring on it is only the beginning!

Dear Reader,

Though all of my stories center around a special romance, I've enjoyed exploring other themes in my books. Family dynamics have always fascinated me, so I've delved into family relationships quite often. In my new trilogy, Proposals & Promises, outside friendships play a big role for all the heroines and heroes.

In this book, *A Reunion and a Ring*, Jenny Baer and Gavin Locke, former college sweethearts, each belong to a close group of friends (several of whom will be popping up in the next two books). Their friends have stood by them through good times and bad, supporting and offering sometimes-too-honest opinions. But how much input should friends have when it comes to romantic choices?

Business owner Jenny is reunited with police officer Gavin as she considers a proposal of marriage from a wealthy, successful attorney who seems outwardly to be her perfect match, unlike Gavin, with whom she has such a passionate—and painful—history. When it quickly becomes obvious that the love they shared never really died, they have to decide whether to play it safe or risk heartbreak again...and their friends have very different opinions about which paths they should choose.

I hope you enjoy reading about the challenging course Jenny and Gavin must negotiate before they find their happy ending as much as I had fun writing it! And I hope you'll join me in the next two books to watch Jenny's friends stumble into unexpected romances of their own.

Gina Wilkins

A Reunion
and a Ring

————

Gina Wilkins

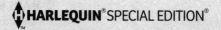

ISBN-13: 978-0-373-65905-0

A Reunion and a Ring

Printed in U.S.A.

 HARLEQUIN®

www.Harlequin.com

Author of more than 100 titles for Harlequin, native Arkansan **Gina Wilkins** was introduced early to romance novels by her avid-reader mother. Gina loves sharing her own stories with readers who enjoy books celebrating families and romance. She is inspired daily by her husband of over thirty years, their two daughters and their son, their librarian son-in-law who fits perfectly into this fiction-loving family, and an adorable grandson who already loves books.

Books by Gina Wilkins

Harlequin Special Edition

Bride Mountain

Healed with a Kiss
A Proposal at the Wedding
Matched by Moonlight

A Match for the Single Dad
The Texan's Surprise Baby
The Right Twin
His Best Friend's Wife
Husband for a Weekend

Doctors in the Family

Doctors in the Wedding
A Home for the M.D.
The M.D. Next Door

Doctors in Training

Prognosis: Romance
The Doctor's Undoing
Private Partners
Diagnosis: Daddy

Visit the Author Profile page at Harlequin.com for more titles.

As always, for my own perfect match—
my husband, John. He proves everyday
that real-life heroes are the ones who are
always quietly there for their family and friends,
whether to lend a hug, a cheer or a hammer
and duct tape. Forever my inspiration.

Chapter One

The headlights sliced through the darkness ahead, glittering off the torrents of rain pounding the windshield of the small car. The wind blew so hard that it took some effort to keep the car on the road. Fingers white-knuckled on the wheel, Jenny Baer leaned forward slightly against her seat belt in an attempt to better see the winding road. The weather had turned nasty earlier than she'd expected when she'd started this almost-three-hour drive.

She'd intended to leave work just after lunch on this Friday, which would have put her here midafternoon, before the rain set in. Instead, she'd been held up with one crisis after another, until it had been after six when she'd finally gotten away. She hadn't even had a chance to change out of her work clothes. She'd thought of waiting until morning to head out, but she'd been afraid she'd only be detained again, maybe until too late to even consider the rare, three-day vacation she was allowing herself.

Her grandmother would say "I told you so" in that sanctimonious tone she often slipped into. Gran had insisted it was foolish for Jenny to take off on her own and stay alone for a long weekend in a secluded mountain cabin. But then, Gran was always trying to tell her only grandchild how to live her life. Though Jenny believed the advice was generally well-intended, she had to remind her grandmother repeatedly that she was thirty-one years old, held a master's degree and was the sole owner of a successful clothing-and-accessories boutique.

Gran would be even less supportive of this private retreat if she knew the reason Jenny had decided impulsively to take it. If she'd told her grandmother that prominent attorney Thad Simonson had proposed marriage, Gran would already be arranging an engagement party, maybe interviewing wedding planners. She wouldn't understand why Jenny had asked for time to think about her answer, though Thad had seemed to consider the request entirely reasonable. After all, he'd said, Jenny's practicality and judiciousness were two of the many qualities he most admired about her. She had accepted the comment as a compliment, as she knew he'd intended—though maybe he'd been just a bit too prosaic about it?

Thad was out of state for a couple weeks on one of his frequent business trips, so Jenny had taken the opportunity to get away for a few days herself. She needed time to think about the ramifications of accepting his proposal without the distractions of constantly ringing phones and never-ending meetings with employees, customers, contractors and sales reps.

Lightning flashed in the distance through the curtains of rain, silhouetting the surrounding hills against the angry sky. The full force of the early-June storm was still a few miles away, but getting closer. What had she been thinking heading into the backwoods with this looming? She was the least impulsive person she knew—at least, that was the way she'd lived for the past decade or so—and yet, here she was, inching through a downpour in the middle of nowhere, heading for a cabin in the Arkansas Ozarks with no housekeeping staff, no room service, none of the amenities she preferred for her infrequent escapes. All with less than forty-eight hours of planning, another anomaly for her.

Considering everything, it was a wonder the cabin had even been available on such short notice, but the too-cheery rental agent had assured her it was ready to rent. Jenny had assumed the weather forecasts had scared off other prospective vacationers, but she'd planned to stay inside to think and work in blessed isolation, so the prospect of a rainy weekend hadn't deterred her. This storm, on the other hand, threatened to be more than she'd bargained for.

She turned onto a steeply rising gravel lane pitted with deep, rapidly filling puddles. The car skidded to the right as she made the turn, hydroplaning on the water beginning to creep over the road. She gasped and tightened her grip on the wheel, letting out her breath slowly when the tires regained traction, digging into the gravel and forcing their way uphill.

She gave a little moan of relief when the cabin appeared in front of her as a darker shape in the headlights. No lights burned in the windows, and there seemed to be no security lights outside. It was hard to tell if the place had changed much since she'd last been here, almost eleven years ago. Lizzie, the rather ditzy rental agent, had explained that there was a carport behind the cabin, but since there was no covered walkway from there to the back door, Jenny parked as close as she could get to the front porch.

Her luggage was in the trunk, but the purse, computer case and overnight bag in the front passenger seat held everything she needed until morning. Arms full, she jumped out of the car and made a mad scramble toward the covered porch. She cursed beneath her breath as she fumbled the key into the lock. Just from that brief dash, her dark hair was soaked, the layers hanging limply around her face and sticking to her cheek. Her once-crisp, white designer blouse was now sodden and transparent, and her gray linen pants were wet to the skin. Mud splattered her expensive sandals and she'd twisted her ankle on the slippery steps. This was what she got, she chided herself, for coming to a place with no eager doorman to assist her.

"I told you so," Gran's imaginary voice whispered in her ear, making her scowl as she shoved through the door.

The interior of the cabin was stuffy and dark, lit only by the almost-constant flashes of lightning through the windows. In the strobe-like illumination, she could see that she had entered a spacious open room with a kitchen and dining area at the far end, and a big stone fireplace on the wall to her right. It was all exactly as she remembered.

She hadn't anticipated the feelings that almost overwhelmed her when she walked in, stealing the breath from her lungs and leaving a dull ache in her chest. She'd told herself she'd sought out this cabin only because it was the first place that had popped into her mind when she'd looked for a peaceful hideaway for the serious deliberations facing her. She'd reassured herself she was drawn here because she'd recalled the natural beauty, the soothing backdrop of birdsongs and mountain breezes. The long Labor Day weekend she'd spent here with her college boyfriend's family had been one of the most pleasant holidays of her life. It had seemed a lucky omen when she'd made a couple of internet searches and phone calls and discovered, to her surprise, that not only was the cabin still on the market for vacation rentals, it was also available this very week.

She'd thought she could enjoy the setting without dwelling on the copious tears she'd shed by the end of that year, after a bitterly painful breakup. She'd thought she had long since dealt with that youthful heartbreak so she could remember the good times and forget the bad, the way any mature adult looked back at the foibles of youth. Maybe she'd even thought this would be a fitting way to put a final closure to her one previous serious relationship before committing completely to a new, permanent union.

Perhaps she shouldn't have been quite so impetuous in booking this cabin. Maybe some old memories should remain locked away, without such tangible reminders.

Shaking her head in exasperation with herself, she set her bags at her feet and fumbled for a wall switch. She hoped the light would banish those old images back into the shadows of the past where they belonged. Nothing happened when she flipped the lever. Great. The storm had knocked out the power. She stood just inside the room, debating whether she should get back in the car and make a break for civilization, preferably someplace new and memory-free. As if in answer, a hard gust of wind rattled the windows, followed by a crash of thunder that sounded like the closest one yet. Okay, maybe she'd stay inside for a while. She tugged her phone out of her pocket, using the screen for light. A very weak signal, she noted in resignation, but the time was displayed on the screen. Almost 10:00 p.m.

She might as well peel out of these wet clothes and try to get a little sleep. Suddenly exhausted, she kicked off her muddy shoes and carried her overnight bag toward the open doorway on the left side of the room. Tomorrow morning, after the tempest had passed, she would decide what to do if the power wasn't restored. She'd anticipated that by the end of this retreat she would have a pile of paperwork completed, crucial decisions made, the rest of her life neatly planned out. Had she been hopelessly naive?

She had her blouse unbuttoned by the time she reached the doorway. She couldn't wait to be out of these wet things and into her comfy satin nightshirt. She hoped the mattress was decent. Not that it mattered much. She was tired enough to sleep on a bag of rocks.

The bedroom was tiny, taken up almost entirely by the bed. Just as that fact registered, she stumbled hard over something on the floor. Her overnight bag fell from her hand and landed squarely on one bare foot. Pain shot all the way up her leg, making her yelp and hop. Her phone hit the floor, screen down, plunging the room into total darkness. She fell onto the bed.

"What the hell?" The sleepy, startled male voice

erupted from the darkness as hands closed around Jenny's arms.

Instinctively, she reached out, and her palms landed on a very warm bare chest sprinkled with wiry hair. She choked out a cry and shoved herself backward. She'd have fallen off the bed if the man hadn't been holding on to her.

"Let go of me!" she ordered sharply, barely suppressed panic making her throat tight. "What are you doing here? I'm calling the police."

"Lady, I *am* the police. And you're breaking and entering."

She struggled to her feet. Holding on to her with one hand, the man sat up on the bed and reached across with his other hand to fumble around on the nightstand. Cold fluorescent light beamed in a small circle from an emergency lantern he'd set beside the bed, making her squint to adjust her vision. Seeing the man who still gripped her arm did not exactly inspire confidence.

His shaggy hair, dark blond with lighter streaks, tumbled around a hard-jawed face stubbled with a couple days' growth of dark beard. She couldn't discern the color of his narrowed eyes, but she could see that his mouth was a hard slash bracketed by lines that probably deepened into long dimples when—or if—he smiled. His bare shoulders were tanned and linebacker broad. Dark hair scattered across his hard chest and narrowed to the thin sheet pooled at his waist. A large white bandage covered his right shoulder, but the evidence of injury made him look no more vulnerable. Overall, she got the immediate first impression of coiled strength, simmering temper and almost overwhelming masculinity.

It took another moment to realize that she knew him.
Or had once known him. Quite well actually. Had his
fingers not been biting into her arm, she might have
thought her weary, memory-flooded mind was playing tricks on her.

"Gavin?"

Surely fate's sense of humor wasn't this twisted!

He blinked up at her and she wondered for a moment
if he even recognized her in the shadows. Though he
didn't release her, his fingers relaxed their grip. "Jen?"

Of all the improbable possibilities she could have
imagined for the start of this poorly planned vacation,
falling into bed with Gavin Locke wouldn't have even
been on her list. She stared mutely at him, unable to
think of a thing to say. Her heart pounded in her chest,
her throat suddenly so tight she couldn't draw air in,
much less force words out. Once again memories filled
her mind in a rush of images so vivid that she could almost feel his hands sweeping over her bare skin, could
almost taste his lips on hers, could almost hear his low,
hoarse groans of arousal and satisfaction.

Even as her face warmed and her pulse raced in reaction to those arousing flashbacks, she struggled to
tamp them down again. She'd simply been caught off
guard, she told herself irritably. It was only natural that
unexpectedly finding Gavin in bed, half-naked, would
remind her of all the times she'd seen him that way
before. Just because she'd long since moved on didn't
mean she'd forgotten her reckless, youthful love affair.
Just as remembering didn't mean she hadn't put it all
safely behind her.

"What are you doing here?" he demanded. "How
did you get in?"

His words roused her into a response, though she wished her voice emerged a little steadier. "I came in through the front door. What are *you* doing here? Did you break in?"

"Did I… No, I didn't break in! I used my key."

Following his sweeping gesture, she glanced toward the nightstand. Beside the plastic lantern sat a couple of medication bottles, a holstered handgun and a metal ring holding several keys. She swallowed, unable for the moment to look away from the weapon.

"Look, Jenny, I'm running on too little sleep, and I'm fairly pissed that someone got all the way into my bed without me hearing a thing, so maybe you could start explaining. Why are you here?" His voice was a growl underlain with steel. It was deeper than she remembered, but his cranky tone was familiar enough. She'd heard it often during the last few weeks of their ill-fated college romance.

She lifted her chin, refusing to be cowed by his mood. "I rented the cabin from Lizzie, the agent at the leasing company. I paid in advance for the weekend, and I have the paperwork to prove it in the other room."

His fingers loosened even more in apparent surprise, and she took the opportunity to snatch her arm away and move a step back from the bed.

He seemed to process her explanation slowly. Perhaps his mind was fuzzy from whatever was in those prescription bottles. "Lizzie rented the cabin to you?"

She nodded. "She said there was a cancelation and that it was available."

"Lizzie is a…"

A clap of thunder drowned out his words. Probably for the best. When the noise subsided a bit, Gavin shook his head, tossed off the sheet and swung his bare legs over the side of the bed. He wore nothing but a pair of boxer shorts. Though she'd seen him in less, that had been a long time ago, and seeing him like this now was not helping to ease the awkwardness of this encounter.

She became suddenly aware that she was standing in front of him with her wet blouse hanging open, revealing the lacy bra beneath. She reached up hastily to tug the shirt closed, fumbling with buttons. Her foot throbbed, she didn't know where her phone had landed and her hair still dripped around her face. In her wildest imagination, she couldn't have predicted her retreat starting out like this.

Seemingly unconcerned with his own state of undress, Gavin stood just at the edge of the lantern's reach. Lightning flashed through the nearby window, revealing, then shadowing, his hard face and strong torso. As inappropriate as it was, considering the circumstances, she still felt a hard tug of feminine response somewhere deep inside her. The years had been very good to Gavin Locke.

She cleared her throat. "If you want to see my paperwork…"

"Come on, Jenny, you know I believe you. Besides, I've dealt with Lizzie enough recently to know that your story is completely plausible."

The wind howled louder outside, so Jenny had to speak up to ask, "Are you saying she rented you the cabin for tonight, too?"

"She didn't have to rent it to me. I own this cabin now."

"Oh, crap." When had he bought it? Why? She had a vague memory of it belonging to an old friend of his family's, but she'd never imagined Gavin would now be the owner.

"You can say that again." He shook his head in disgust. "I told Lizzie not to rent the place this week, that I needed it myself. I should have known she'd get it mixed up. She's new at the job and she's incompetent."

"I…" A gust of wind blew so hard she could feel the cabin being buffeted by it. Something hit the roof above them and she cringed, glancing up instinctively. She couldn't help thinking again of the tall trees surrounding the place. She suspected a branch had just fallen on the roof, and she hoped it wouldn't be followed by the whole tree.

Gavin looked up, too, and then staggered, as if doing so had made him dizzy. He put out a hand to steady himself and nearly knocked the lantern off the nightstand. Without thinking, Jenny moved to steady him, her hands closing over his shoulders. He flinched away from her grip on his bandaged shoulder, and it was obvious that she'd hurt him. Even as she snatched her arms back, she realized that his skin had seemed unnaturally warm.

Frowning, she reached out again, this time laying her palm tentatively against his cheek. She tried to keep her touch relatively impersonal, merely that of a concerned nurse. "You have a fever."

He brushed her off. "I was sleeping. I'm probably just warm from that."

"No, it's definitely a low-grade fever. Is your shoulder wound infected?"

"I'm taking antibiotics," he muttered.

"Since when?"

"Since this morning. Saw my doc before I drove up

from Little Rock. He said it's not too bad and the meds will clear it up soon."

She stepped back. "Have you taken anything for the fever?"

"I'm fine."

"I've got some aspirin in my bag. Maybe you should lie back down while I try to find it. If I could borrow the lantern?"

One hand at the back of his neck, he stared at her. "You broke in here to take my temperature and give me aspirin? Are you sure my mother didn't send you?"

Oddly enough, the mention of his mother made her relax a bit. She had always liked his mother. "I didn't break in. And I'm leaving immediately. I apologize for the misunderstanding. Do you want the aspirin before I go or not?"

Looking steadier, he scooped up a pair of jeans from the floor and stepped into them. She noticed only then that she'd tripped over a pair of his shoes. He must have pretty much stripped and fallen into bed earlier. If he'd taken a pain pill beforehand, that could explain why he'd slept so heavily he hadn't heard her entrance over the noisy weather.

He swung an arm in the direction of the single window in the little bedroom. The glass rattled in the frame from the force of the wind blowing outside, and a veritable fireworks exhibit played across the slice of sky visible from where she stood. Thunder had become a constant grouchy roar, as if the night itself was grudgingly surrendering to the storm.

"You aren't going back out in that. The way that rain's coming down, I wouldn't be surprised if the road is flooded. And the full force of the storm hasn't even hit yet. We're in for worse before it passes."

She thought of the water already creeping over the road when she'd approached the cabin. That frightening moment when she'd hydroplaned. She swallowed. "I'll be fine," she said, wishing she sounded a bit more confident.

She bent to retrieve her dropped phone just as Gavin took a step toward her. "Don't be foolish. The storm is too…"

The collision knocked her flat on her behind and nearly caused Gavin to sprawl on top of her. Somehow he steadied himself, though it involved flailing that made him grunt in pain from his injured shoulder.

Sitting sprawled at his feet, she shook her head. Could this ridiculous evening get any worse? Or was she tempting capricious fate to even ask?

Gavin was beginning to wonder just what was in those pills he'd taken before he'd turned in. Was he hallucinating? Or had a gorgeous, wet woman with a smoking body revealed by an open blouse really fallen out of the storm and into his bed? A woman right out of the memories he thought he'd locked away long ago, though they'd escaped a few times to haunt his most erotic dreams. Was he dreaming again now?

No. The way she sat on the floor glaring up at him told him this was no fantasy. The dream-Jenny had been much more approachable.

Muttering an apology, he reached down to haul her to her feet with his good arm. He released her as soon as he was sure she was steady on her feet.

"It wasn't your fault," his uninvited guest conceded.

"I was picking up my phone. I dropped it when I stumbled over your shoes."

Which made it still his fault, in a way, but he wasn't going to get into a circular argument with her. "Are you expecting anyone else to arrive tonight?"

Was he unintentionally intruding on what she'd planned to be a romantic, rustic retreat? He told himself the possibility annoyed him only because he didn't want to have to deal with yet another intruder. What other reason could there be after all these years?

"No. I was going to hide out here alone for a few days to get some work done without interruptions."

He was still having trouble clearing his thoughts. He couldn't begin to understand why Jenny had come to this particular place to work. What the hell was he supposed to do with her now?

An unwelcome recollection from the last time they'd been together here slammed into his mind in response to what should have been a rhetorical question. He could almost see himself and Jenny, naked and entwined, lying on a pile of their clothes in a secluded, shaded clearing. Laughing and aroused, they'd made good use of the stolen hour. His blood still heated in response to the distant echoes of their gasps and moans.

Shoving the memories fiercely to the back of his mind, he half turned away from her. The storm assaulting the windows made it obvious she wasn't leaving immediately. He released a heavy sigh. "Maybe you remember there's another bedroom at the back of the cabin, behind the kitchen. You can crash there tonight, and we'll get this all figured out in the morning."

"Spend the night here? With you?"

Pain radiated from his shoulder, and his head was

starting to pound. He hadn't had a full night's sleep in a couple days. Patience was not his strong suit at the best of times, but he'd lost any semblance of it tonight.

"I didn't suggest sleeping in the same bed," he snapped. "The other room has a lock on the door. Use it, if you're so damned afraid of me. Hell, take my weapon and sleep with it under your pillow, if it makes you feel better."

She sighed and shook her head. "I'm not afraid of you, Gavin."

"Great. I'm not afraid of you, either."

A soft laugh escaped her, sounding as if it had been startled out of her. "You're in pain," she said. "I'll get the aspirin."

"I had a pain pill before I went to sleep. Probably shouldn't take aspirin on top of it."

"Oh. You're right. How long has it been?"

"Couple hours, maybe. I can take one every four hours, but I don't usually need them that often."

"What did you do to your shoulder?"

"Long story." And one he had no intention of getting into at the moment. "There's another emergency lantern in the kitchen. I'll help you find it. I'm thirsty, anyway."

"Thank you."

He saw her glance up nervously when something else hit the roof, and he wondered if she was anxious about the storm. He remembered that she'd never been a fan of storms. Yet, she'd been prepared to go back out in it? He shook his head.

Carefully pulling on a loose shirt, he picked up the lantern and moved past her toward the doorway. He heard her pick up her bag and hurry after him, trying to stay close to the light. He retrieved the second fluorescent lantern from the kitchen counter, pushed the power button, then turned to offer it to his visitor. She accepted with barely concealed eagerness.

He could see her more clearly in the double lantern light. She'd been very pretty just out of her teens, but the intervening decade had only added to her attraction.

Her dark hair, which she'd once worn long and straight, now waved in layers around her oval face. He remembered how it had once felt to have his hands buried in its soft depths.

Her chocolate-brown eyes studied him warily from beneath long, dark lashes. There had been a time when she'd gazed at him with open adulation.

She was still slender, though perhaps a bit curvier than before. He'd once known every inch of her body as well as his own, and he noted the slight differences now. He tried to stay objective, but he was only human. And she looked damned good.

Her expensive-looking clothes were somewhat worse for wear after her jog through the rain. He wasn't one to notice brands, but even he recognized the logo on the overnight bag she carried. Apparently she had achieved the success she had always aspired to.

He hadn't kept up with her—quite deliberately—but his mother had mentioned a few months ago that she'd seen Jenny's photo in the society section of the local newspaper. She'd watched his face a bit too closely as she'd commented casually that Jenny had been photographed at some sort of community service awards dinner for Little Rock's young professionals. She'd added that Jenny was reported to be dating a member of one of central Arkansas's most prominent and long-established families. He'd answered somewhat curtly that he read the sports pages, not the society gossip, and that he had no particular interest in who his long-ago college girl-friend was now dating. He wasn't sure he'd succeeded in convincing his mother that Jenny never even crossed his mind these days.

So what had really made this country-club princess choose to vacation at his rustic fishing cabin? As unlikely a coincidence as it was, he had no doubt that she was as dismayed to have found him here as he was that she'd shown up so unexpectedly. The genuine shock on her face had been unmistakable.

He reached into a cabinet and drew out a glass. "Are you thirsty? I doubt there's anything cold in the fridge, but I can offer tap water. Or I think we've got some herbal tea bags. It's a gas stove, so I can heat water for you, if you want."

Despite the circumstances, he was trying to be a reasonably gracious host, though he wasn't the sociable type at the best of times. After all, it wasn't Jenny's fault the agency he'd hired to rent out the cabin had recently employed a total airhead. He'd have more than a few pointed words for someone there tomorrow.

Hal Woodman, an old friend of his father's, had built this cabin on the Buffalo River as a fishing retreat and rental property when Gavin was just a kid. Hal had let Gavin's parents use it frequently for family vacations. A few years later, Gavin's dad bought the cabin from his then-ailing friend. Gavin and his sister inherited the place when their father died a couple years ago. His sister lived out of state now with her military husband, so Gavin had bought her portion. To defray the costs, he rented it out when he wasn't using it—which was more often than he liked because of his work schedule.

The cabin was close enough to hiking trails, float trip outfitters and a couple of tourist-friendly towns that it rarely sat empty for long. Yet, had anyone suggested that Jenny Baer would be one of his weekend renters, he would have labeled that person delusional.

Jenny shivered a little, and he realized her clothes were still damp. Hell, she'd likely sue both him and the leasing agency if she got sick. "Go put on some dry clothes. I'll heat some water. The bathroom's through that door."

Jenny hesitated only a moment, then tightened her grip on the lantern and turned toward the bathroom. Grumbling beneath his breath, he filled the teakettle and reached for the tin of herbal teas his health-conscious mom had insisted he bring with him. She was still annoyed with him for taking off to heal in private rather than letting her nurse him back to health from his injury, which would have driven him crazy. He disliked being fussed over, even by the mother he adored.

Jenny wasn't gone long. When she returned, she wore slim-fitting dark knit pants with a loose coral top that looked somewhat more comfortable than her previous outfit. She'd towel-dried her hair and her feet were still bare, but other than that, she could have been dressed to host a casual summer party. Had she really packed this way for a cabin weekend alone? He had to admit she looked great, but out of place here. No surprise.

He set a steaming mug of tea on the booth-style oak table. A bench rested against the wall, and four bow-back chairs were arranged at the ends and opposite side of the table, providing comfortable seating for six adults. He brought friends occasionally for poker-and-fishing weekends, and the family still tried to gather here once a year or so, but usually he came alone when he needed a little downtime to recharge his emotional batteries.

Setting the lantern on the table, Jenny slid into a chair and picked up the tea mug, cradling it between her hands as she gazed up at him. "I'm really sorry about this mix-up. And that I woke you so abruptly when I'm sure you need sleep."

He started to shrug his right shoulder out of habit, then stopped himself at the first twinge of protest. "Not your fault," he said again. "How long were you planning to stay?"

She looked into her mug, hiding her expression. "I paid for three nights, which would let me stay until Monday afternoon if I'd wanted."

"By yourself." That still seemed odd to him. Was she still seeing Mr. Social Register? Or had there been a breakup? He couldn't help thinking back to the weeks following his breakup with Jenny. He'd dropped out of college and holed up here alone for a couple of weeks, until his parents had shown up and practically dragged him back into the real world. He'd entered the police academy as soon as he could get in after that, putting both the pain and the woman who'd caused it out of his mind and out of his heart. Or at least that's what he'd told himself all these years since.

Still, just because he'd retreated here after a split didn't mean Jenny's reasons for being here were in any way the same.

No particular emotion showed on her face when she spoke, still without looking up at him. "I've gotten behind on some business and personal paperwork and I thought it would be nice to have a little time to myself in peaceful surroundings to tackle it all. I needed a chance to concentrate without constant interruptions, and it's usually hard to find that back at home."

Leaning against the counter, he raised his water glass and murmured into it, "I know that feeling."

She glanced at him from beneath her lashes. "You're getting away from everyone, too?"

"In a way. I, um, had surgery on my shoulder last week and I'd rather hide out and heal alone rather than be hovered over by my mom."

Her full lips curved then into a faint smile. "From what I remember about you, that doesn't surprise me at all."

He didn't want to discuss memories, good or otherwise.

"So you drove straight here from Little Rock?"

"Yes. It wasn't storming when I left. I had hoped it would hit later, or maybe skip this area completely."

She looked up when thunder boomed again, louder and closer. "Thor's really angry tonight," she murmured with a wry, somewhat nervous-looking smile.

A chuckle escaped him. "The myth or the superhero?"

"The myth, of course." She gave a husky little laugh that echoed straight from those memories he was trying so hard to hold back. "And the superhero. I've seen all the movies, even though my, um, friend calls them cheesy. Don't get me wrong, I enjoy more intellectually challenging films for the most part, but I…"

She stopped herself with a grimace. "I'm sorry, I'm babbling. This whole situation is just so…awkward."

"Yeah." He set his glass beside the sink, his attention lingering reluctantly on her mention of a "friend."

Something about the way she'd said the word made him wonder...

He motioned abruptly toward his bedroom. "I'm going back to bed. Make yourself at home. We'll sort it all out in the morning. You'll be getting a refund, of course, for anything you've paid up front."

Lightning zapped so close to the cabin he could almost smell the ozone. The near-deafening clap of thunder was almost simultaneous. He saw Jenny flinch, her hands visibly unsteady around the mug. Wind-driven rain hammered the windows, and he thought he heard some hail mixed in. The full force of the storm had definitely arrived.

"Do you know if we're under a tornado warning?"

He shook his head. "My phone would sound an alarm if we were. It's only a severe thunderstorm warning."

"You'll let me know if it turns into anything more?"

"Of course."

He took another step toward the bedroom just as another barrage of hail hit the roof and windows. Hearing a sound from Jenny, he looked over his shoulder. She sat at the table holding her mug, her face pale in the circle of lantern light. She made no move toward her own bedroom. "Are you okay?"

She glanced his way. "I hope this hail doesn't damage my car."

His truck was under cover in the carport, but he wasn't about to offer to go out and swap places with her. He figured she had insurance. "Maybe the hail won't last long."

"I hope you're right," she said, her voice almost drowned out by thunder. The storm was so loud now it seemed to echo inside his aching head.

Raising his left hand to his temple, he said, "Let me know if you need anything."

"Thanks. I'm okay for now."

Nodding, he turned and headed grimly for the bedroom, thinking he'd better lie down before he embarrassed himself by falling down. He'd been assured the wound infection was not serious and should heal quickly with a five-day course of antibiotics, but combined with everything else, it was kicking his butt tonight. He could only blame that for his inability to think clearly about the woman now sitting at his table.

He'd been far too rattled ever since she'd tumbled out of the storm, out of the past and into his bed.

Jenny watched Gavin walk away. His thin shirt emphasized the breadth and muscularity of his shoulders and arms. His well-worn jeans encased a tight butt. At thirty-one, he'd put on a few pounds since she'd seen him last, but those pounds were all muscle. She saw no evidence of his injury from the back, which only enhanced the impression of strength and power. She waited only until his bedroom door closed sharply behind him before she sagged in her chair and hid her face in her hands.

She had always wondered how she would feel if she saw Gavin again. She'd hoped she would have enough warning to brace herself. As it was, it had taken every ounce of control she could muster to hide her shock and dismay at finding him here.

Gavin had certainly shown no particular emotion, other than the initial, understandable confusion when he'd first recognized her. Since then, he'd given no evidence that he viewed her as anything more than an annoying intrusion. Remembering how angry he'd been when she'd broken up with him, she supposed that shouldn't surprise her.

She felt suddenly alone in her little circle of lantern light. A crash of wind and thunder made her jerk, almost spilling the dregs of her tea. She swallowed, squared her shoulders and stood to carry the cup to the sink.

Retrieving her bag and the lantern, she moved into the back bedroom, which was even smaller than the one in which she'd found Gavin. A full-over-full bunk bed was pushed against the wall, leaving little walking room. She'd forgotten about the bunk bed. Just over ten years ago, on that pleasant Locke family getaway, she and Gavin's sister had slept in this room. His very traditional parents had taken the bedroom and Gavin got the sleeper sofa.

Which hadn't prevented her and Gavin from sneaking off a few times to be alone, she recalled with a hard swallow. They'd found one particularly inviting clearing in the woods, carpeted with soft moss, serenaded by the sound of lazily running water.

The unsettling memory was so clear she could almost hear that water now. She took a step forward into the room and started when her bare foot landed in a puddle of cold water. Lifting the lantern, she discovered a steady stream of rain pouring in onto the top bunk. Another, smaller leak dripped onto the floor where she'd just stepped.

She raised the light higher, looking up at the ceiling. Another surge of hail pounded the windows and more water gushed through the leak above the bed. Obviously, shingles had been loosened or blown off. She rushed back into the kitchen, set her bag on the table and began to rummage quickly in the cupboards for containers in which to catch the leaks. Maybe she could save the wood flooring if she intervened quickly. She tried to be quiet, but pans clattered despite her efforts. She pulled out the largest pots she found, then tried to juggle them with a couple of dish towels and the lantern. This no-electricity thing could get old very fast.

The other bedroom door flew open. "What are you doing out here?" Gavin sounded both sleepy and irritated.

"I'm sorry I disturbed you again," she replied over her shoulder. "The roof in this bedroom is leaking in two places. I'm trying to catch the water before it does any damage."

"Well, hell."

Moments later, he knelt beside her with another towel, though she'd already mopped up most of the standing water. His now-bare shoulder brushed her arm as they reached out together, and she felt a jolt of electricity shoot through her. Just static, she assured herself, scooting an inch away. She stuck a pot beneath the leak and heard the rhythmic strike of drops against metal.

"Should we try to move the bed away from the leak?"

"Nowhere to move it to." He picked up the other pot and set it on the top bed. Now the water splashed in stereo, thumping against the pots like miniature drumbeats. "There are waterproof covers on both mattresses. I'll strip the beds and try to dry everything tomorrow."

He turned toward her, his partially shadowed face inscrutable. "Obviously you can't stay in here. That dripping would drive you nuts."

"True."

He let out a sigh and motioned toward the doorway. "Looks like you're sleeping in my bed tonight."

Her heart gave a hard thump simultaneously with the loud clap of thunder that accompanied his words.

Chapter Two

Jenny woke with a start Saturday morning at the sound of a closing door. Disoriented, she blinked her eyes open, only then remembering that she'd spent a restless night on the sleeper sofa in the cabin's living room. Gavin had offered the use of his bed, but she'd refused. She wouldn't displace an injured man from his bed because of a mix-up that was no fault of his own. Not to mention that the thought of crawling into sheets still warm from his body had been disconcerting enough to make her toes curl.

Though the fold-out mattress was comfortable enough, she hadn't slept well, and the noisy storm had been only part of the reason. She'd lain awake for a long time trying to come to grips with the reality that after all these years her ex-boyfriend lay only a few feet away. Old memories—some bittersweet, some wrenching—

had whirled through her head, leaving her too tense to relax. It had simply never crossed her mind that she might run into Gavin at the cabin she'd only visited before with him. Some might say there was a complicated Freudian explanation behind her decision to come here to consider another man's proposal, but that was ridiculous. It had been the peace and quiet that had drawn her here, certainly not nostalgia.

Gavin stood in front of her when she turned her head toward the front door. Dressed in a gray T-shirt, jeans and boots, he was damp and mud-splattered. He pushed a hand through his wet hair, which was so long it touched the back collar of his shirt, indicating he'd missed a couple of cuts. He still hadn't shaved, adding to his roguish bad-boy appearance. Her pulse jumped into a faster rhythm at the sight of him. If she'd had any doubt that she still found Gavin strongly attractive, that question was answered definitively now.

"Sorry I woke you," he said.

Self-conscious, she swung her feet to the floor and pushed herself upright, trying to smooth her tousled hair. It bothered her to think he'd walked right past her as she'd slept, leaving her feeling uncomfortably vulnerable. That was a little hard to deal with this morning.

Light filtered in through the windows. She could hear rain still falling on the roof, though the height of the storm had passed. She saw no lights burning inside, so she assumed the power was still out. "What time is it?"

"A little after eight."

Later than she usually slept, but she hardly felt well-rested. "What's it like out there?"

His response was blunt. "A mess. Lots of limbs on

the ground. There's a big tree over the road a few yards from the house, totally blocking the drive, and I'm sure there's flooding beyond that. You're lucky you got here when you did last night. You won't be leaving for a while yet. No way to get down the hill in your car."

Not promising. She moistened her dry lips before asking, "Is my car damaged?"

"A few hail dings. You were fortunate. A good-size limb fell only a couple feet away from your hood."

While she was relieved her car hadn't sustained damage, she wasn't sure *fortunate* was the right word to describe her current situation. "How long do you think it will take for them to clear the tree from the road?"

"Them?"

"The county? Highway department? Whoever does that sort of thing."

"Highway department doesn't take care of rural gravel roads. And the tree's on private property, so the county isn't going to deal with it. I'm sure they have their hands full elsewhere. From what I saw on my phone news feed, there was quite a bit of damage around this part of the state last night."

"Oh." She swallowed, feeling suddenly a bit panicky at the thought of being trapped here with Gavin for much longer. It wasn't that she feared for her safety— but she couldn't say the same for her peace of mind. "So, what are we going to do?"

"I've got a chain saw in the back of my truck. I was planning to do some light trimming and clearing this weekend, anyway, assuming my shoulder cooperated. I'll tackle the tree when the rain stops, but it's going to take a while with only the one sixteen-inch saw. As for the flooding, you'll just have to wait for that to recede.

There's too much water over the road for you to risk driving through it, even if you could figure out a way to get around the tree. You'd be swept into the river before you made it across."

Unsurprised that he hadn't planned to let his injury stop him from the work he'd wanted to do, she twisted her fingers in front of her. "How long do you think it will take for the flooding to recede?"

He glanced upward, silently indicating the still-falling rain. "This county remains under a flash flood alert. It's going to take a few hours for all the water to drain off once the rain stops."

"Have you heard from home? Was there storm damage in the Little Rock area?"

He shook his head. "The worst of the storms were confined to this part of the state."

She was relieved that her family and her business had escaped the brunt of the storms she'd so foolishly driven into, but she wasn't looking forward to spending several hours alone here with Gavin and their shared memories. "Surely I can get out somehow. Is there a back road, maybe?"

"Look, Jenny, I'm no more pleased about this than you are, but you might as well face facts. You'd be risking your life to try to make it down that hill now."

She sighed and pushed her hair out of her face, silently conceding his point. At least he wasn't pretending to be delighted to have her here. If there was one thing she remembered about Gavin Locke, it was that he had always been bluntly, sometimes painfully, honest.

"You had planned to stay for three nights, anyway," he reminded her. "It's not as if you have anyplace else you need to be today."

"True. But I had expected to be here alone."

"I'll try to stay out of your way."

"That's not what I meant. I'm the one who's intruding."

He made a dismissive gesture, though he didn't assure her that it was no bother to have her here. They both knew better.

"At least let me cook breakfast," she said, deciding to attempt to act as dispassionate as he was about the situation. "I brought a few nonperishable groceries with me. The bags are out in my car. I was going to try to find a market for some fresh food if I decided to stay the full three days, but I…"

"I have food," he broke in curtly. "The kitchen's stocked. Help yourself to anything you find in the cabinets or pantry. I doubt there's anything salvageable in the fridge. I'm not hungry, but I'd take coffee if you want to make it while I wash up. There's a French press in the cabinet by the stove."

"Are you still running a fever?" She resisted an impulse to step forward and touch his face. He hadn't seemed to like that last night. It was probably best to keep the touching to a minimum, anyway, while they were stranded here together.

"I'm fine."

She wasn't sure she believed him entirely, but figured it would be a waste of time to argue. Or even to point out that a man with an injured shoulder probably shouldn't be out in the rain clearing storm debris.

He disappeared into his bedroom. After folding away the sleeper sofa and neatly stacking the sheets and pillows, Jenny rummaged in the kitchen. She filled the kettle with water and when it boiled she made the coffee, then two bowls of instant oatmeal she found in the pantry. A few bananas were turning brown on the counter, so she sliced a couple on top of the oatmeal and set the steaming bowls and mugs on the table. She'd just taken her seat when Gavin joined her again. He hadn't changed, but he'd tried to clean the mud splatters on his clothes, leaving damp, streaked spots behind. She had to glance quickly down at her oatmeal to hide any hint of the feminine appreciation that flooded unbidden through her again. She was really going to have to put a stop to this, she thought irritably.

"I said I'm not hungry." He dropped into his chair and studied the oatmeal with a scowl, proving himself to be just as grouchy as she was feeling. Was it possible he was dealing with some of the same unwelcome emotions she was trying to suppress?

She shrugged and answered with outward nonchalance. "Don't eat it, if you don't want it. I'll have yours for seconds. But it's there if you think you need to fuel up before doing any work outside today."

After a moment, he heaved a gusty sigh and picked up his spoon. "Fine."

She smothered a smile by stuffing a spoonful of oatmeal and bananas into her mouth. After washing it down with a sip of the passable coffee, she tried to ease the tension between them with small talk. "When did you buy the cabin?"

"My dad bought it nearly seven years ago. When he died five years later, I ended up with it."

She replied with genuine sympathy. "I'm sorry. I didn't know about your dad. He was a good man."

Gavin nodded. "He was."

"How's your mother?"

"She's well, thanks. Yours?"

"Still working as a nurse in a hospital in Little Rock." Her mother had liked Gavin, and had been openly disappointed when Jenny broke up with him.

"And your grandmother? Still living?"

Her grandmother, on the other hand, had not approved of Gavin, and the antipathy had been reciprocal. Jenny could still hear the faint edge of resentment in his voice, though the question had been civil enough. She focused on her breakfast when she said, "Still feisty as ever."

He responded to that understatement with a grunt.

Maybe that subject was a bit too touchy still. She changed it quickly. "How's Holly?"

"Married to an air force pilot. They've got two boys, Noah and Henry, six and four. They're living in Illinois at the moment. Scott Air Force Base."

An only child herself, Jenny had always been somewhat envious of the warm relationship Gavin had with his older sister. They'd gotten along amazingly well for siblings. During the time Jenny had spent with them, there had always been friends of Gavin's and Holly's around, usually engaged in good-natured but fierce competitions—basketball or softball or flag football, or spirited board games indoors. The memory of all that fun and laughter made her throat tighten as she studied the unsmiling, hard-looking man across the table. It had taken a lot worse than a college breakup to leave those dark shadows within his navy eyes.

"How do you like being an uncle?"

She was pleased to see a shadow of his old grin flit across his firm lips. "The boys tend to think of me as an automatic treat dispenser. Tug at my jeans and candy magically emerges from my pocket. Holly says it's a good thing I don't see them often or she'd have to put a stop to it. As it is, she turns a blind eye. She knows I won't overdo it. And I always get them to work up a sweat to burn off the extra sugar."

An image of him roughhousing with two cute little boys distracted her for several moments. As prickly as he could sometimes be with adults, Gavin had always liked kids, and the feeling had been mutual. She would bet he was the kind of uncle who would roll in the dirt with his nephews, let them climb all over him, sticky fingers and all.

Thad would be more likely to teach his nephews, if he had any, to play chess. Which would also be quite cute, she assured herself quickly, feeling a vague, totally unjustified ripple of guilt course through her, as if she'd been disloyal.

Gavin changed the subject. "What are you doing these days?"

"I own a fashion and accessories boutique in Little Rock."

"What's it called?"

"Complements."

He nodded. "I've heard of the place. Someone I dated briefly shopped there a lot."

"That's good to hear. That she liked my store, I mean."

He chuckled drily. "She complained about the high prices, but she still shopped there enough to max out her credit cards."

"We carry high-end merchandise," Jenny replied without apology. "Designer items that can't be found in the local department stores."

"Yes, well, it's been a year or so since I've seen her, but I'm sure she's still a loyal customer."

Judging from his dispassionate tone, she doubted he'd been particularly invested in the relationship. If the woman was a regular patron at Complements, it was entirely possible Jenny knew her, but she had no intention of asking him. It was none of her business who Gavin had dated since she'd last seen him. Nor if he was dating anyone seriously now. Just as she saw no reason to discuss Thad with him.

He pushed away his empty bowl and picked up his coffee cup. "So you accomplished your lifelong goal. You own your own successful business. I assume you obtained an MBA, as well? That was always the plan, wasn't it?"

She felt her chin rise in instinctive irritation, and she lowered it deliberately, keeping her expression composed. "Yes. I'm planning to open a second store in the next few months. I love my work."

Which was absolutely true—and another reason she was having trouble deciding whether to accept Thad's proposal, she thought somberly. Marrying Thad would change her life significantly. Though he'd always expressed his respect and admiration for her business achievements, he'd been quite candid about what he was looking for in a life partner. Supporting his political aspirations was high on his list of attributes in a mate. To keep up with the demands of that undertaking, she'd either have to sell her business eventually or at the very least turn over most of the daily operations to employees. After spending so much time tenaciously building her clientele and reputation, it was hard to contemplate putting Complements in the hands of anyone else.

None of which she was going to discuss with Gavin, of course. She sipped her rapidly cooling coffee, then set the cup on the table. "So, you did what you wanted, as well. You became a police officer."

She hadn't forgotten that he'd once wanted that career more than he'd wanted her. She wouldn't lie to herself that there wasn't still a little sting to the memories, but she hoped she'd hidden any remaining bitterness.

He nodded. "Went back and earned a degree in criminal justice, too. I took night classes and online courses when I was off-duty. Made my dad somewhat happier, anyway."

Both Gavin's parents had been educators. Neither had been pleased when he'd decided at an early age that he wanted to be a police officer. Their objection hadn't been the social status or modest pay scale of police—which had been the bluntly stated basis of her grandmother's disdain for the job—but rather the danger and unsavory situations in which their son would spend many of his working hours. They'd made no secret that they'd hoped he would change his mind while he obtained his college degree.

Jenny had met him in a sophomore sociology class. The attraction had been immediate and powerful. After they'd started dating, she'd added her arguments to his parents', trying to convince him to channel his interest in criminal justice into a less dangerous profession. At first, he'd seemed to concur and begun to study for the law school entrance exam, to put away bad guys as a prosecutor rather than an officer. Truthfully, she'd been aware of his underlying lack of enthusiasm for that career path, but in her youthful optimism, she'd been sure he would learn to like it.

On the very rare occasions when she had looked back at their eighteen-month-long relationship through the viewpoint of a more mature adult, she'd realized it was probably his feelings of being pressured into a career he didn't want that had made him turn sullen and difficult. He must have felt as if his own desires were always being disparaged and discouraged. He'd quarreled more and more often with his parents, and with her. He'd accused her of being so obsessed with her own ambitions, of trying so hard to please her grandmother, that she was willing to sacrifice their relationship to achieve her aims.

Maybe her lofty goals didn't include being married to an ordinary cop, he'd snarled. Maybe the reason she kept urging him to go to law school had been more for her own ambitions than for his. During the ensuing years, she'd wondered uncomfortably if there had been some grain of truth in his allegations. She'd always assured herself that, like his parents, she had worried more about the risk and uncertainty of a police officer's work rather than any lack of social status. She had witnessed her own mother's grief after being widowed at a young age by a charming, daredevil firefighter, who'd been as reckless off-duty as on the job and had died in a drag-racing accident. Having struggled with that gaping loss herself, Jenny hadn't been able to deal with the thought of losing the man she loved in the line of dangerous duty. The image still made her blood chill.

She'd been unable to convince Gavin exactly how upsetting that possibility had been to her. They'd had one last, fierce quarrel in which they'd both said very hurtful things, and that had been the end of their romance. The emotions had been too raw, the anger too hot, to allow them an amicable parting. A week later, she'd been shocked to learn that Gavin had left the university, only three semesters short of graduation. She assumed he'd entered the police academy soon afterward, though she'd never heard from him again. She had thrown herself into her studies, shedding her tears in private and burying the pain as deeply as possible, rarely to be acknowledged since.

Maybe Gavin's thoughts, too, had drifted back to their painful breakup, because before she could reply, he shoved his chair back abruptly from the table. "I'm going to start on that tree. Thanks for the breakfast."

"You should take care with that shoulder."

He merely gave her a look and walked out, leaving her shaking her head in exasperation. While Gavin had changed in many noticeable ways since she'd last seen him, it was obvious that he was still as stubborn as ever.

The rain had dwindled to little more than a cool mist while he'd been inside. Gavin tossed damp hair out of his face and lifted the chain saw from the back of his truck with his good arm. Pulling the starter was going to be a challenge, but he'd manage. The sooner he cleared that tree out of the way, the sooner he or Jenny or both of them could get away from here. And the sooner there would be an end to those uncomfortable catch-up conversations.

Why the hell had he felt the need to tell her he'd gotten his degree? He'd heard himself blurting it out almost before he'd realized it. That damned degree didn't make him any more worthy, as far as he was concerned. Jenny could have a dozen advanced degrees and own a

Fortune 500 company, and he would still take pride in the uniform he donned every working day.

He remembered vividly the way Jenny's grandmother's lip had curled when he'd mentioned his intention to enter the police academy after finishing college. Lena Patterson had made it quite clear that she had higher aspirations for her granddaughter than to align herself with a "low-level civil servant." Having known by then that Jenny's father's death had left them grief-stricken and financially burdened, Gavin had decided that Lena Patterson was a pompous, bitter woman. She had channeled her personal disappointments into her bright, beautiful and motivated granddaughter, pushing Jenny toward higher education and a socially and economically advantageous marriage.

The old woman had done a damned good job of programming her granddaughter from a very early age. He'd seen the way Jenny lit up in response to Lena's sparsely doled praise. That had been hard for him to compete with at twenty-one. He doubted he could do so even now, if he were inclined to try.

He set the chain saw beside the other tools he'd already gathered around the fallen tree and stepped back to analyze the project. The oak was big. The uptilted root ball came almost to his shoulder. A tangle of leafy branches covered the driveway in a dense barrier. Even with two good arms, this tree would require hours to remove.

His phone buzzed in his pocket and he removed one bulky work glove to draw it out, sighing when he saw his mother's number.

"I'm fine, Mom," he said without giving her a chance to say anything.

She laughed softly, unperturbed by his sardonic tone.

"I'm glad to hear it. It sounds as if your area got hit hard by last night's storms."

"Lost a couple of trees, a bunch of limbs. Couple leaks in the back bedroom I'm going to have to patch. Other than that, no real damage done."

"I heard there was flooding up that way."

"There's flooding down the road, but just a few wet patches up here on the hill." His dad had always said that the river would have to be at hundred-year flood stages to creep up to the cabin.

"Can you get out?"

"Not yet, but the water should go down fairly quickly once the rain finally stops." He hoped the road would be dry enough for safe travel by the end of the day, though the heavy cloud cover did not look promising. He wouldn't be surprised to be drenched again at any minute.

"How's your shoulder? Is the infection better?"

"Better. No fever today."

"I'm glad to hear it. Now, please use common sense and try not to overdo it with the storm cleanup. I know better than to try to make you promise not to tackle any of it today."

"I won't overdo it."

"I worry about you being up there all alone when you haven't been out of the hospital for a whole week yet. I know you don't like being hovered over, but I wish you'd stayed a bit closer to home for at least a few more days."

"Gavin, do you have an extra pair of work gloves I can use?" Jenny called from behind him before he could reassure his mom again. "I'd be glad to help you clear this… Oh. I'm sorry." Spotting the phone in his hand, she grimaced in apology.

He should have known his too-perceptive mother wouldn't miss a beat. "Gavin? Someone is there with you? Is it anyone I know?"

There was no way he was telling her at the moment about his ex-girlfriend's presence. His mom had liked Jenny back in the day, even though she'd reacted in true overprotective mama-bear mode when Jenny broke up with him. She'd insisted that Jenny had broken her son's heart. Gavin wouldn't have phrased it quite that way. Then again, he couldn't really argue it, either.

"I have to take care of some things around here before the rain starts again," he said into the phone, ignoring her questions. "I'll call you later, okay?"

He heard her sigh, but his mother surrendered to the inevitable. No doubt she'd grill him good later, face-to-face. "Fine. Just…take care of yourself, will you?"

"Bye, Mom."

He disconnected the call and shoved the phone back into his pocket before turning to Jenny, studying her through the clear plastic protective glasses. She'd changed into a T-shirt and jeans. She'd pulled her hair into a loose ponytail. Beads of fine mist already glittered within the dark strands. Trendy, neon-green running shoes not at all suited to muddy manual labor encased her feet.

She held up her perfectly manicured hands. "I'm sorry, I didn't realize you were on the phone. I'm looking for an extra pair of work gloves so I can help you."

"I can handle this."

"It will go faster if I pitch in."

He wasn't so sure about that. She could prove to be more of a distraction than a help. But he could think of no way to decline the offer without coming across as a jerk. If he tried too obviously to avoid her, she might even think he'd never quite gotten over her.

He cocked his chin toward the back of the house. "Extra work gloves and safety glasses are behind the seat in my truck. It isn't locked."

He figured she'd tire out quickly and head back inside. Until then, he would keep her too busy to reminisce.

He had the chain saw running by the time she returned wearing the too-large, leather-and-canvas gloves and an oversize pair of plastic safety goggles. He'd deliberately waited until she was out of sight to fire up the saw so she wouldn't see him wince and curse when he pulled the starter cord. He had no intention of showing her how much discomfort he was in—not actual pain, but that would probably set in before the day ended. Didn't matter. He wanted this road cleared as quickly as possible.

Because the saw was so noisy, he communicated with shouts and hand motions, instructing her to stay at a safe distance while he cut, after which she could drag the smaller pieces off the road and into the ditch. Considering her formidable resolve, he supposed he shouldn't have been surprised that Jenny threw herself into the job. It was dirty and sweaty work, but she pushed on gamely until her ponytail straggled against her damp neck, her clothes were muddy and her shirt had a small tear at the hem, perhaps from catching on a sharp branch. And still he had to force himself to concentrate on the potentially hazardous job at hand when his eyes wanted to turn in her direction instead. Even tousled and grubby—or perhaps especially so—something about her made his thoughts wander into dangerous and forbidden directions and brought back memories that heated his blood and hardened his groin.

Didn't mean anything, he assured himself. He was a reasonably healthy male in the middle of a dry spell, so it was only natural for him to react to an attractive, temptingly tousled woman.

After two hours, she looked as though her energy was fading fast. He felt as though he'd been kicked in the shoulder by an angry horse. Turning off the saw, he set it on the ground and swiped at his sweat-beaded forehead with the back of his left hand. He'd removed several of the large limbs, but a few more needed to come off before he could even attempt to move the tree off the road. It was taking longer than he wanted to cut through the hard wood. He only hoped he had enough gas and oil on hand to finish the job.

He still needed to figure out a way to pull the tree out of the roadway, but maybe he could think more clearly after taking something for pain. He knew better than to swallow prescription pills and then run a power saw, so he'd settle for over-the-counter remedies. He glanced at Jenny. "You need a break."

Even muddy, wet and wilted, she could skewer him with a lifted eyebrow. "*I* need a break?"

"*We* need a break," he conceded grudgingly.

She nodded in satisfaction. "I just want to move this last branch."

She took hold of a leafy limb the size of a small tree and gave a tug. It didn't budge. Gavin stood beside her, grabbing the branch with his left hand. Their gloved hands almost touched. He had only to shift his weight a little to be pressed against her from behind. She glanced up at him over her shoulder and their eyes locked. Hers dilated a bit; his probably did, too.

He told himself again that some reactions were purely biological. And then quickly slid his hand down a couple inches from hers, ostensibly to get a better grip. "On three."

With his count, Jenny pulled so enthusiastically he nearly fell backward when the branch shot forward. He put one foot back to steady himself, and reached out automatically with his right hand to get a better grip. A grunt of pain escaped him before he could swallow it. He hoped Jenny hadn't heard, but he should have known better. She didn't say anything, but he saw the sympathy on her face when he glanced at her.

He turned away. The one thing he had never wanted from Jenny Baer was pity. "Let's go inside."

Gavin insisted Jenny take the bathroom first to get cleaned up while he put on the kettle for tea. He was still making an effort to be a thoughtful host, she thought. Smiling a little, she closed herself in the bathroom, then glanced into the mirror. Her smile faded immediately. She reached hastily for a washcloth and a bar of soap.

When she rejoined Gavin in the kitchen, she spotted a bottle of over-the-counter pain relievers by the sink that hadn't been there earlier. His shoulder had to be giving him fits, but he hadn't complained once and she didn't think he wanted her to ask.

"Thank you," she said, accepting the mug he offered her. The tea was still too hot to drink, so she carried it to the table and took a seat to wait for it to cool a bit.

"I checked the weather on my phone. Rain's moving

this way again, but maybe this round will pass through quickly."

"I hope so."

Gavin moved toward the bathroom, carrying his mug with him. "I'm going to wash up. Make yourself at home."

She waited until he was out of sight before she let out a sigh and allowed her shoulders to sag. Spending time with Gavin was both easier than she might have expected and harder than it should have been. She'd come here to make decisions about her future and instead had been slapped in the face by her past. Wasn't that ironic?

Needing a distraction, she reached for her phone. The signal was weak, but there was no one in particular she wanted to call. She'd texted her mother and Thad to let them know she'd arrived safely. She hadn't mentioned that she wasn't alone in the cabin. That had been a bit too complicated to explain to them by text or a quick, static-filled call.

When Thad traveled, he called every evening at 6:00 p.m., so reliably that she could set her clock by his ring. It was an arrangement they'd worked out together as a way of managing their equally hectic schedules, making sure they didn't miss connections. "Their thing," Thad called it teasingly. He'd phoned at that time yesterday, just as she was trying to get away for the drive here. He hadn't hidden his concern about her solitary vacation, but he'd added that he hoped she had a relaxing few days and returned ready to make plans for their promising future together.

She'd always appreciated that Thad respected her choices, though sometimes she wondered fleetingly if it was mostly because his own life was so busy that he hardly had time to think about her issues. Still, he went out of his way to find time for their calls, proving he was willing to make compromises in their potential marriage, which was certainly important to her. After all, she and Gavin had broken up partially because neither had been willing to compromise their disparate goals and dreams. Wasn't that only further evidence that a relationship based on logic and respect was more reliable than one based on passion and emotion?

She refused to answer. She'd been stubbornly resisting the unhappy memories her surprise reunion with Gavin had stirred up, and she certainly wasn't going to sit here brooding about the past now. She focused more fiercely on her phone. The signal was strong enough to allow her to access her email. There weren't many to deal with. Amber, her assistant, was taking care of the business for now. She read her text messages and saw a note from her long-time good friend, Stephanie "Stevie" McLane, checking to make sure she'd survived the storms. She typed a confirmation and received an immediate response.

Bored yet?

Jenny smiled wryly. Hardly, she typed.

Thought you'd have your fill of rustic isolation by now.

Not as isolated as I expected, she returned.

Meaning?

After hesitating for a few moments, Jenny drew a breath and replied, Gavin Locke is here.

No way!

That was pretty much how she'd expected Stevie to react. She could clearly imagine her friend's blue eyes rounded with shock. Stevie had been her staunchest supporter after the split with Gavin, though Jenny had always wondered if her friend secretly considered the breakup a mistake.

Her phone beeped to announce another text. Did you know he'd be there?

Of course not.

Details, girl.

Will call later. She wanted to make that call only when she was certain Gavin wouldn't overhear.

What about Thad?

Jenny frowned as her fingers tapped the screen. What about him?

Does he know?

Jenny moistened her lips before entering her answer. Nothing to know. Not like I planned it.

She bit her lip as she read Stevie's answering text. How does Gavin look?

He looks… Jenny gave it a moment's thought before typing good.

Still single?

Far as I know. Call you soon, okay?

You'd better.

"If you're trying to make a call, you'll get better service outside." Gavin nodded toward her phone as he ambled back into the room. "I usually sit on the porch swing for clearer reception."

Jenny set her phone aside. "Thanks, but I was just texting with Stevie. Do you remember her?"

"Of course. She was your best friend in college."

"Still is."

"Did she marry that guy she was dating? The drummer?"

Funny. Jenny had almost forgotten the drummer. She suspected Stevie had, too. "No. They broke up not long after... No."

For some reason, she was reluctant to even refer to her breakup with Gavin.

"She's still in Little Rock?"

"Yes. She's dating another musician," she confided with a faint smile. "A bass player this time."

When it came to romance, Stevie was nothing if not an optimist. Yet Jenny had been increasingly aware that Stevie hadn't said much about Jenny's deepening relationship with Thad. She wasn't sure why. She'd have thought Stevie would agree that Thad appeared to be Jenny's ideal Mr. Right. He was handsome, wealthy, successful, socially secure. A junior partner in his family-connected, long-established law firm, Thad was already being courted by political-party bigwigs. He was considering a run for state representative in three years, and had already made a few trips to Washington to meet with some big shots there. Everyone they knew—their families, their friends, their associates—seemed to consider them the perfect couple.

Yet, oddly enough, rather than being as enthusiastic as Jenny might have expected, Stevie had been somewhat restrained in her encouragement for the match. Was Stevie too wrapped up in her own romance, or did she have some doubts about Thad that she wasn't sharing? Did she question whether Jenny would ever truly be happy in a partnership based on considerations other than what Stevie would consider epic romance?

Sure, Thad was a confirmed workaholic who sometimes became so immersed in his ongoing projects and future goals that he tended to forget about everyone and everything else, but then Jenny had always been type A herself. She didn't need a man's constant attention. She genuinely liked Thad and she enjoyed his company when they found time to be together. She was sure they'd get along quite nicely as they built a satisfying future together. Why shouldn't that be enough?

Realizing impatiently that she'd allowed her thoughts to wander again, she glanced at her watch. "Should we eat something before we go back out? Are you hungry?"

Gavin shook his head. "That next round of rain's not going to hold off much longer. I'll try to get some more clearing done while I can."

She stood and moved toward the cupboards. "I spotted packages of peanut-butter crackers in here. At least eat some of those to protect your stomach from the meds." She opened a door and motioned toward a top shelf, just above her head. "It was always your favorite snack."

He moved behind her to reach the carton. The action

brought them very close together. All he'd have had to do was lower his arm to wrap it around her shoulders. She'd have moved aside, but the counter was in the way. Any move she made would only brush her against him. Instead, she froze in place, almost holding her breath until he stepped back, the carton in his hand.

"You remember my fondness for these, do you?"

Able to breathe again now that there was a bit more distance between them, she laughed softly, grateful it came out relatively steady. "How could I forget? You stashed them in your car, in your backpack, in your dorm room, in my dorm room. Your friends used to joke that you should buy stock in a cracker company. I'm just a little surprised you haven't gotten tired of them by now."

His mouth quirked into a faint smile as he shrugged. "I don't eat them as much as I used to, but they're still a pretty good snack."

She watched him rip into a cellophane packet, her smile feeling more natural as an amusing memory occurred to her. "Remember when your sister's little white poodle tore into a whole carton while we were outside watching July Fourth fireworks at your parents' house? We came back inside to find paper and cellophane and crumbs everywhere and the poor dog had peanut butter smeared all over her face. Holly got hysterical thinking her pet was going to die, but fortunately the dog got more in her fur than her belly."

Gavin chuckled wryly. "Mom insisted on rushing the dog to an emergency animal clinic, just in case. We were going to have homemade ice cream after watching the fireworks, but it had all melted by the time the

crisis was over. You know, that dog lived to be fifteen.
Just died a couple years ago."

"What was its name again? I can't remember."

Gavin made a face. "BiBi. I can't forget because it
ran off from Mom's house one day when she was dog-
sitting while Holly was out of town, just before Christ-
mas. Mom called me in tears. I had to drive slowly
around her neighborhood in my cruiser, calling the stupid name from my open window. 'Here, BiBi. C'mere,
BiBi.' I felt like an idiot. It was sleeting. Took me an
hour to find the half-frozen mutt, and then it had the
nerve to pee on me when I picked it up."

She couldn't help laughing. He'd have hated every
minute of that episode—but for his mother and sister,
he'd have done it with only token grumbles. "That is
too funny."

"Glad you think so," he muttered, though his lips
twitched.

For a moment, she was swept back again to the early
days of their romance, which had been filled with laughter. Her smile faded as she returned abruptly to the
present. Leaning casually against the counter, Gavin
gazed down at her, his eyes gleaming in the shadowy
light. She felt the hairs on her arms rise, as if the air
between them charged suddenly with static. She really
needed to stop those mental flashbacks before they got
entirely out of control.

Did Gavin sense the change, as well? His eyes narrowed, and even the hint of amusement vanished, leaving his face carved again into hard, inscrutable lines.

He grabbed a couple more packets of crackers and
turned away. "I'm going back out. Rest awhile, if you
want. I can handle things out there."

She released a long, unsteady breath when the front door closed behind him. Wow, that had turned quickly. She'd just been reminded all too vividly of how quickly the laughter in their youthful relationship had dissolved into tears. She was annoyed to realize the memories could still sting, even after all these years, even after she'd long since assured herself she was over it.

She was tempted to stay safely inside while he continued the cleanup. Because that made her feel cowardly, she lifted her chin and refused to give in to the impulse. She reached for her borrowed work gloves and headed for the door. The sooner the road was cleared, the sooner this blast from the past would be over.

Chapter Three

Almost an hour later, most of the branches were off the tree trunk and dragged to the side of the road. Jenny felt her muscles protesting the hard labor, and she suspected she would be sore tomorrow. She kept a close watch on Gavin, noting his face grew tighter as their work progressed. He was obviously favoring his right arm, certainly making an effort not to exacerbate the injury, but she could tell he was hurting and that he was overdoing it regardless. Yet, he'd tried to assure her he could handle this on his own. Right.

They were both panting after dragging and shoving yet another limb into the now-full ditch. Jenny wasn't sure if the moisture on her face was due more to perspiration or the mist that was beginning to fall more heavily now, making the ground slick beneath her sneakers. She slid on a patch of leaves, did a little flailing dance, then planted her heels firmly in the dirt to anchor herself. Gavin applauded, his sawdust-covered gloves thudding dully together. She smiled and bobbed a careful bow in his direction. His long slash of dimples appeared briefly, then vanished when he turned back to the tree.

"Now what?" she asked, motioning toward the huge trunk still completely blocking the narrow gravel road.

"Now that the trunk is light enough not to yank the bumper off my truck—I hope—I'm going to try to hook a chain to it and pull it out of the way, at least enough for us to get around it. Once I can drive past it, I'll go down and check the flooding at the foot of the hill. As long as the rain holds off a while longer, maybe we..."

The sky opened. It was the only way to describe the way rain dumped suddenly onto them, as if someone had turned on a showerhead full blast above them. Gavin snatched up the chain saw and followed Jenny's mad dash to the covered porch, but both of them were soaked by the time they ducked under the overhang.

"Are you *kidding* me?" She shoved her sodden bangs out of her eyes, shaking her head in dismay. "Could this weather get any crazier?"

Gavin ran a hand through his wet, shaggy hair, spraying raindrops around his feet. "It's spring in Arkansas. Crazy weather is pretty much expected this time of year. They've been predicting these storms for a couple weeks now."

"I know," she admitted with a sigh. "I just hoped the worst forecasts would be wrong. They often are, you know."

He leaned back against the wall of the cabin, gazing out at the downpour without answering. An occasional windblown gust of rain blew in at them, but they were already so wet it didn't seem to matter. Actually, the wet breeze felt rather good after the sweaty work. She settled into a damp rocker and watched a rivulet of water slide down a porch post.

His gaze focused intently on the falling rain, Gavin spoke quietly. "You're not getting much of your paperwork done today. Didn't you say that's why you came?"

She shrugged. Once again, she had a perfect opening to tell Gavin exactly why she'd needed some time to herself, but once again, she decided to let the opportunity pass. She told herself it would just be too awkward to discuss Thad with Gavin, especially considering she hadn't even given Thad an answer to his proposal yet. "I'll find some time later, once I get off this hill."

"You make a habit of taking off on your own like this to work?"

That made her laugh, though without much humor. "This is the first weekend I've not spent at my office in longer than I can remember. And I very rarely have time just to myself. This trip was an aberration in almost every way—and wouldn't you know, it would turn out to be a disaster."

"Sorry you were disappointed."

Realizing she might have sounded a bit ungracious, she shrugged. "You had no control over the weather. And the booking mix-up wasn't your fault, either. Just all-around bad luck."

Because that didn't sound much better, she added, "I mean, it's very nice seeing you again, it's just…"

"Jenny." His tone was dry, and she figured he must find her sudden discomfiture amusing. "It's okay. You didn't hurt my tender feelings. And it's nice to see you again, too. Sort of."

Because she understood exactly what he meant by that, she gave him a quick, wry smile. "Yeah. Sort of."

He didn't return the smile. "Always figured we'd run into each other again someday, both still living in the area and all. I'm kind of surprised it took so long. Guess we hang in different circles these days."

She was determined to act as nonchalant as he appeared to be. "It's funny that we reconnected here, three hours from where we live."

"Not so strange, I guess, since I own the cabin and you were looking for a secluded place. Maybe the fact that you remembered it so well is a little odd."

"I hadn't thought about it in years," she assured him quickly. "My assistant unintentionally reminded me of it when I jokingly said that I needed to crawl into a cave or something for a few days to think and get organized and she said maybe I should find a nice, secluded mountain cabin. This place popped into my head and I did an impulsive internet search and…well, here we are."

"Here we are."

She twisted her fingers in her lap. "It's nice that we can be…" *Friends* didn't seem to be quite the right word. She quickly substituted, "Civil."

"Why wouldn't we be civil? We dated as kids. We went our own ways. It's been—what, a decade or so? Life's gone on, for both of us."

It had been ten years and two months since they broke up. Not that there was any reason to get that specific, but she couldn't help wondering if he, too, remembered the exact date. Still, as he said, they'd been very young. A lot had happened since for her, and certainly for him, too. She was in a relationship, and for all she knew, he could be, too. Neither had been pining for the other all these years. There was no reason at all they couldn't be...well, friendly. She couldn't see them hanging out as buddies. Not because of any difference in social status, but because she suspected there would always be undercurrents between them that made their interactions too potentially volatile.

As if to reinforce that thought, Gavin pushed away from the wall with a bit more force than necessary. "I'll be right back."

Jenny was torn between enjoying the sound of the rainfall on the porch roof and being impatient for the rain to end so they could get back to clearing the road. She glanced behind her. Gavin had left the door ajar, probably to allow fresh air into the stuffy rooms. It was quiet inside the dim cabin. She didn't hear him moving around at all.

Curious, she stood and walked inside, leaving her muddy shoes on the doorstep beside his boots. She had just moved farther into the room when she heard a heavy thud and a heated curse from Gavin's bedroom.

Tentatively, she headed that way. "Gavin? Are you all right?"

His bedroom door was open. Shirtless, he stood in front of the dresser mirror, an open first aid kit in front of him, the bandage on his shoulder hanging crookedly. A plastic bottle of isopropyl alcohol lay on the wood floor beside his feet; fortunately, the lid was still on so it hadn't spilled.

"Do you want some help changing that bandage?" she asked, deliberately offhanded. "I'm sure it's a little hard to do with your left hand."

"I've managed before. Just knocked the bottle off the

dresser with my elbow. I usually change the bandage in the bathroom, but the light's somewhat better in here."

"I didn't say you couldn't do it yourself. I said I'm here to give you a hand, if you'd like. If you'd rather handle it yourself, fine."

After only a momentary hesitation, he nodded. "It would be faster if you help. Uh, thanks."

Because she knew what it probably cost him to accept assistance from her—from anyone, really, being such a fiercely independent sort—she wasn't bothered by his somewhat less than gracious acceptance. "Maybe you should sit down so I can reach it better. Does it need to be cleaned? Should I bring a washcloth?"

"It's not dirty. The bandage was wet and uncomfortable, so I thought I should swap it for a dry one."

"Makes sense." She reached for the half-removed bandage and eased it away from his injury. With an effort she kept her expression impassive when she saw the jagged, six-inch row of close-set stitches that marched across his shoulder. The skin around the threads was puckered, but the redness didn't seem to be spreading and his shoulder wasn't hot to her touch, so the meds must be working.

"Are you supposed to put antibiotic ointment on the stitches?"

Sitting on the end of the bed, he nodded toward a tube on the dresser. "Just a little. Only reason I wear the bandage is to keep my shirt from rubbing the stitches."

Using a square of gauze, she dabbed ointment lightly over the wound. Their heads were so close she felt his warm breath on her cheek.

Did he lift weights these days? When she'd known him before, he'd been slender and athletic, but the muscles in his arms and chest hadn't been quite as well-defined. He was definitely a man in peak condition despite the injury. And if her fingers lingered for a moment on a taut bicep—well, that could be attributed to incidental contact while she prepared the area for the new bandage.

The shadowed room was silent except for the soft splash of rain on the windows. She was all too aware of the rumpled bed, the masculine clutter of clothes and toiletries, the mounting warmth in the air. She felt a need to fill the quiet, though she would try not to slip into nervous prattling. "You said you had surgery on your shoulder? Did you tear a ligament or something?"

"Something like that."

The very blandness of his nonreply made her hands go still. In a flash, she was taken back to her childhood, watching her mom patch up the latest injury her dad had acquired in one of his reckless stunts, either on the job or off. Just as it had when she was an anxious child, her stomach knotted painfully.

"You weren't, um, shot, were you?" she asked, voicing the worst nightmare that had haunted her when Gavin announced his determination to don a badge.

"I wasn't shot."

And that was all he was going to tell her. He couldn't have made it clearer if he'd said it outright.

Taking the less-than-subtle hint, she bit her lip and finished applying the bandage without speaking again. She smoothed tape over the clean gauze, taking her time to make sure the edges were well sealed. Her hand still resting on his shoulder, she glanced at his face to make sure she wasn't hurting him, only to find him looking gravely back at her. For a fleeting moment, she saw

in his eyes a hint of the Gavin she'd once known—
younger, more open, less hardened by his job and experiences.

Her breath caught hard in her throat as more memories crashed through her mind in a kaleidoscope of
broken images. Hungry kisses. Heated caresses. Nights
of passion more overwhelming than anything she'd experienced before. Or since, for that matter. Which was
totally understandable, right? Wasn't it supposed to be
that way when a woman's thoughts drifted back to her
first love?

The shadows seemed to deepen in the room around
them, enclosing them in a cozy corner of soft light spilling in through the single window. Her gaze lowered
slowly, pausing on his mouth. His lips looked so stern
and firm, yet she remembered them as warm and eager.
If she allowed herself, she suspected she could still re-
call their taste. It was probably—definitely—best if she
kept that memory locked away along with all the others.

His voice was rough when he broke the silence. "That
should do it."

"What? Oh." Realizing he referred to the bandage,
she dropped her hand and stepped quickly back. "Yes,
that should hold."

"Jenny…"

A heavy pounding on the front door made them both
start and turn in that direction. Jenny heard someone
shouting, a muffled male voice calling Gavin's name.
They hadn't locked the front door. She heard it open,
heard the voice more clearly. "Gavin? Hey, buddy, you
in here? You okay?"

"Rob." Shaking his head, Gavin pushed himself to
his feet and called out, "I'm here. Hang on."

Snatching up a dry T-shirt, he moved toward the bedroom door without looking back at Jenny. She followed quickly. It occurred to her that if someone had made it up the road to the cabin, that meant she could now drive down. It was probably only because she was so tired that she wasn't more excited by that realization.

Rob Lopez peered around the cabin door, squinting into the shadows as he called out again. "Hey, Gav? Are you— Oh, there you are."

Pulling the T-shirt over his head, Gavin moved to greet his friend. He was surprised to see him there. His pals had a standing invitation to join him whenever he was using the cabin, but usually they called before showing up. "Hey, Rob. What are you doing here? How'd you get past the flood and the downed tree?"

Rob opened the door all the way, shaking water out of his curly dark hair like a wet labradoodle as he stood just outside on the porch. "I won't come in—my boots are too muddy. We drove up in J.T.'s off-road rig. Nearly floated it at the bottom of the hill. You have two trees uprooted, by the way. There's another a quarter mile down the road. I left the other guys working down there, and I hiked up to let you know we're here—in the rain, I might add, though it's almost stopped now, at least for a little while. You're going to owe me for this one."

"Other guys?"

"Yeah. J.T. and— Oh. Hello." Rob was looking over Gavin's shoulder and it wasn't hard to guess what, or rather who, had brought the look of surprised speculation to his face.

Belatedly realizing that donning his shirt as he'd entered Rob's field of vision might have given him the wrong idea about what he and Jenny had been doing in the bedroom, Gavin cleared his throat. "Rob Lopez, this is Jenny Baer. Jenny and I knew each other back in college. Long story, but Lizzie at the leasing office screwed up and rented the cabin to Jenny for the weekend. Jenny didn't expect to find me here when she arrived in the middle of the storm last night."

Rob's eyebrows lifted. "Well, that's awkward. Is that your car out front, Jenny?"

"Yes." If she was at all uncomfortable, it didn't show in her polite expression when she moved fully into the room. "I arrived just ahead of the worst part of the storm. Gavin allowed me to sleep on his couch last night and I've been trying to help him clear the drive today."

Rob glanced from her to Gavin and back. "He put you on the couch? What's wrong with the back bedroom?"

"Roof's leaking," Gavin grumbled. "Lost a few shingles in the storms last night. I was going to work on that after I got the trees out of the road. Power's out, too."

Rob nodded. "We can help with the roof. Looks like you've made good progress on the near tree. Won't take long to haul it out of the way, assuming the next wave of rain holds off long enough."

Feeling increasingly disoriented, Gavin pushed his left hand through his hair. "You want to tell me what y'all are doing here?"

With a shrug, his friend answered lightly, "Impulsive road trip. We heard about the storm damage in this area. There wasn't any destruction to deal with in our part of the state, so we figured you could use an extra hand— or six—with cleanup here. You being short a hand of your own and all. We didn't know you already had a very nice pair of hands up here helping out."

Rob winked at Jenny as he spoke. The way she smiled in response made it clear that the woman who'd been so notably composed during the past few hours was not immune to Rob's notorious charm. Gavin felt his brows drawing into a scowl, and he deliberately smoothed his expression. It wasn't his business if Jenny fell for Rob's overused lines.

He moved abruptly toward the door. "I left my boots and gloves on the porch. Jenny, now that the guys are here to help, there's no need for you to come back out. You can just rest in here for now."

Reaching up to tidy her ponytail, she crossed the room behind him. "Actually, I'd just as soon help rather than sit in here in the dark. My tablet and phone are getting low on power, so I can't really work, anyway."

He had no good argument. He certainly couldn't tell her he found her presence too distracting while he tried to work.

"Whatever you want to do." Without looking back at her again, he all but pushed past Rob to step out onto the porch and reach for his boots.

"Easy, bro," Rob murmured with a low chuckle. "A guy might think something—or somebody—has got you all hot and bothered."

Gavin shot his friend a look that made Rob back off quickly with both hands raised and a devilish twinkle in his dark eyes.

Rob watched as Jenny perched on the edge of a porch chair to lace on her bedraggled, once-bright sneakers. "Hate to tell you this, but I think those shoes might be goners," he said. "Doubt they'll ever be clean again."

She wrinkled her nose. "I've pretty much figured that out already. I didn't think to bring work boots with me."

"I told you it wasn't necessary for you to slog through the mud with me this morning," Gavin felt compelled to point out. "But I'll pay for the shoes, anyway, when I refund your rental money. None of this was your fault."

Pulling the second lace tight, she stood and reached for the muddy gloves she'd worn earlier. "Of course you won't pay for my shoes. Don't be silly."

Something about her tone made him scowl again. Had she just brushed him off? He glared after her as she walked down the steps with Rob, but she didn't glance back. With a grumble, he snatched up the chain saw and followed.

"Big tree," Rob commented unnecessarily as they approached the fallen oak. "You got a lot of it cut up this morning."

"I figure I can drag the rest of it out of the way with my truck. There's a heavy chain and a few more tools locked in the utility shed behind the cabin."

Rob nodded. "Might be better to hook it up to J.T.'s heavier rig. They should have the other tree out of the road pretty quick. It's not nearly as big as this one. They were dredging out the ditches at that low spot with shovels, too, to help the water run off faster."

"Maybe I should take that branch off while we wait." Gavin motioned toward the one he meant. "If the trunk rolls when we try to move it, that one could dig in and give us problems."

"Agreed. But why don't you let me cut it? That shoulder's got to be giving you fits by now."

Actually, the pain was a heck of a lot worse than that, but he didn't want to admit it. Especially in front of Jenny. "Fine, you cut the limb while I get the chain. It's too bulky to carry, but I can bring it around in the back of my truck. Jenny…"

"I'll help Rob." Donning her safety glasses, she moved into position to grab hold of the branch after it was cut. As he turned to head around the side of the cabin, Gavin could already hear Rob chatting with Jenny as if they were old friends. But then, Rob had never met an attractive woman he didn't like. An impressive percentage of them liked him in return.

He wouldn't have thought Rob was Jenny's type. An EMT Gavin had met in the line of duty a few years ago, Rob was hardly in the same league with the guy his mother said Jenny had dated—and was possibly still seeing. But whatever.

Feeling increasingly grumpy and blaming it on the weather, his discomfort and his weariness, he shoved his hand into his pocket to retrieve the key to the utility shed. All in all, the best thing he could do now was to focus on the tasks at hand. He'd deal with his unexpected visitors—all of them—as best he could during the process.

It didn't take Rob long to cut through the branch Gavin had pointed out. Jenny realized only then how much Gavin had been held back by his injured shoulder. Remembering the stitches that had marched across his taut skin, she bit her lip. He must be terribly uncomfortable, to say the least, though he would fall over face-first before he would admit it. Even as a young man, he'd hated acknowledging when he was sick or hurting. She'd once teased him of being afraid testosterone would leak out of his ears if he confessed to any weakness. She could still remember the way he'd grinned, kissed her and murmured, "You're my only weakness, Jen."

Breaking into the painful memory, Rob planted his foot on the tree trunk and snapped off a smaller branch with his hands. He tossed it in the ditch on top of the others. "Sounds like a pretty harrowing night. You're lucky you made it here safely through the storm."

"I was foolish to be out in it. I didn't pay close enough attention to the weather reports."

He eyed her over another fallen branch he'd just picked up. "Were you planning to do some fishing while you were here?"

She laughed softly at the image of herself handling a squirming fish. "No. It was just supposed to be a private work retreat."

Didn't other people feel the need occasionally to get away, to find a quiet place alone to think and plan and evaluate? True, it wasn't something she had done before, but it had made sense to her when the idea had occurred to her. Gavin had had a similar plan; he'd holed up here to rest and heal in peaceful privacy. The weekend hadn't worked out as either had expected obviously.

Casting a lingering look around at the sodden landscape, Rob said, "Couldn't ask for a more peaceful place for a hideaway, normally. Gavin's been really generous letting me come up here when I needed to get away and if the place wasn't already rented out. I've spent quite a few pleasant hours sitting on that porch in the dark, drinking a cold beer and listening to the frogs and crickets."

"That was my plan," she said with a wistful smile. She hated beer, but she mentally substituted a cup of tea and was sorry she would miss the experience. "Of course, it wouldn't have worked out even if it hadn't been for the storm. Once I'd discovered Gavin was using his cabin and it had been leased to me by mistake, I'd have left immediately and found another place to stay for the weekend."

"I doubt he minded sharing for one night," Rob murmured just as Gavin parked his truck nearby and climbed out with a slam of his door.

Gavin reached into the back of the truck and started to lift a chain, but he dropped it almost immediately. The metal links clanked against the truck bed, not quite drowning out his muttered curse. Apparently he'd unthinkingly used his right arm and the heavy chain had hurt his shoulder. Instinctively, she moved toward him to help, but Rob cleared his throat softly, stopping her midstride. Without looking their way, Gavin switched arms, grabbed the chain with his left hand and hauled it out of the truck, dropping it at their feet. Hefting another branch, Rob acted as though he'd noticed nothing.

Hearing the roar of a motor, Jenny looked around to see a heavy-duty rig powering up the muddy hill. With an extra set of oversize wheels on the back, an extended cab and a row of floodlights across the top, the truck looked made for hauling, towing and chewing up rough terrain. It stopped just short of the downed tree, and two thirtysomething men climbed out. The driver was well over six feet tall, black, broad-shouldered and male-model handsome, the passenger shorter, ginger-haired and built like a linebacker. Gavin definitely hung out with the athletic crowd, but then he always had. As a matter of fact, he'd been hanging out with the redhead for quite a long time, she realized.

Avery Harper glanced curiously in her direction as he and his companion approached. He stopped suddenly in his tracks. "Jenny? Jenny Baer?"

She pushed a wet strand of hair out of her face. "Hello, Avery. It's nice to see you again."

Green eyes wide with shock, Avery looked from her to Gavin and back again. "Wow. Are you two...? I mean... Wow."

"Jenny didn't know I was here when she drove up last night." Gavin sounded weary, as if he had already grown tired of explaining. She could understand. How many more times were they going to have to recount, both together and separately, how they'd ended up spending a night together in his cabin? He finished giving the quick summary of last night's events to his friends, introduced J. T. Dennett to Jenny, then barely gave them time to exchange hellos before launching into his plan for clearing the drive.

Feeling somewhat in the way, she moved back as the four men attached a chain to the fallen tree and then connected it to the tow hitch on J.T.'s truck. She noticed that Gavin's friends did most of the heavy work, nudging him out of the way to keep him from overusing his injured arm. They weren't particularly subtle about it, but were so casually jovial that he took no offense.

"Better stand back," Avery advised, moving to Jenny's side when J.T. climbed behind the wheel of the truck. "Just in case."

Together they moved a few feet backward while Gavin and Rob stepped off to the other side to call out directions to J.T.

"So, you didn't know Gav was here," Avery commented a little too blandly.

"No," she said firmly. "Not a clue. And he had no warning that I'd rented the place."

"Huh. I have to admit, I was surprised to see you here, but his explanation made sense, even if it was a crazy coincidence."

"Well, I'm glad you found it believable," she said drily.

His nod had a slightly mocking edge. "More believable than if he'd announced the two of you had gotten back together," he murmured.

Her relationship with Avery had been rather acerbic while she'd dated Gavin. He probably liked her even less since the breakup. But that was okay. She didn't have to try to make Gavin's friends like her anymore, though she was getting along well enough with Rob.

Still, it was only polite to try to make conversation. "So, Avery, are you still on the force with Gavin?"

Avery had actually entered the academy a year earlier than Gavin, and Jenny had blamed him for having so much influence over Gavin. At the end, Gavin had snapped at her that he knew his own mind, made his own choices and wasn't just following his friend's lead. He'd actually set law enforcement as a career goal even before Avery, he'd informed her defensively.

Avery nodded in response to her question. "Different division, but yeah, still a cop. Made sergeant a few months back. And I got married last fall. My wife's a dispatcher for the department. She's on duty today."

She tried to inject a measure of genuine warmth into her smile. "Congratulations on both your promotion and your marriage."

Not notably disarmed, Avery nodded again. "Thanks. Gavin's still catching up after he quit for more than a year, but he'll be promoted soon himself. Wouldn't be surprised if he eventually makes captain before I do."

"Um, he quit?" she asked casually.

"Yeah, when he… Oh, he hasn't mentioned it to you."

"We haven't talked much since I've been here. Last night we were dealing with the storm and the leaks, and today we've been trying to clear the drive, so there hasn't been a lot of catching up."

She wondered why he'd quit, what he'd done instead, why he'd gone back—all questions she had no business asking. It was obvious Avery had clammed up now and would be revealing no further tidbits about his friend's current life.

After unhooking the chain from the now-out-of-the-way tree, the men stood around the trunk arguing the best way to cut it for firewood. They all agreed they should tackle the leaking roof first.

"I've got some extra shingles in the utility shed," Gavin said.

Jenny felt a fat raindrop splash against her cheek. Swiping at her face, she turned to Gavin. "Now that the road's clear, maybe I should leave before the bottom falls out again."

All four men spoke at one time, and all with some variation of "no."

"You haven't seen how much water is over the road down there," J.T. explained, motioning with one hand. "To be honest, it was pretty stupid for me to drive through it, even in my rig. That lightweight little car of yours would never make it."

Deflated, she sighed. "So how long do you think it will take for me to be able to get out?"

J.T. glanced at Gavin. Both shrugged.

Avery scowled up at the dripping sky. "It would help if this damned rain would stop. Now that we've cleared out the ditches down there, the water should go down pretty quick once they stop refilling with rain. Even then we're talking about a couple hours before the road would be completely safe."

Rob nodded and winked comically at Jenny. "I'd rather you wait until it's safe. It's my day off. As pretty as you are, I'm still not in the mood to administer CPR today."

"Rob's a compulsive flirt, but you should know he's an EMT," Avery said so quietly to Jenny that she wasn't sure anyone else could hear. "Just another lowly civil servant who doesn't move in your social circles. I doubt you'd be interested in him."

A little gasp of indignation escaped her. Had Avery just blatantly accused her of being a snob?

Before she could retort, Gavin surged forward, planting himself in front of his friend with a glare of warning. "Jenny is my guest here," he said in a low but unyielding voice. "I expect her to be treated courteously. Is that clear, Avery?"

Avery had the grace to look a little sheepish as he muttered, "Sorry, Jenny."

Biting her lower lip, she nodded to acknowledge the halfhearted apology. The inexplicable acrimony between her and Avery had come between Gavin and his pal on several occasions back in college. She certainly wouldn't want to cause a rift between them now. As unfair as the remark had been, she couldn't entirely blame Avery. He was just watching out for his friend.

"Hey, Avery, help me carry this cooler and stuff," J.T. shouted from his truck, seemingly unaware of the tension between the trio. "We might as well dig into the sandwiches and beer we brought until the rain stops again."

Avery turned and walked away without looking back. Clearing his throat, Rob followed quickly.

"I'm sorry, Jen," Gavin said quietly. "I'll talk to Avery."

She shook her head. "No, that's not necessary. He has a right to his opinions of me. Even though they're wrong."

She didn't expect to have to deal with Avery much longer, anyway. And she was perfectly capable of defending herself, if she had to. He'd simply caught her off guard this time.

"You know, I have driven in bad conditions before," she said, turning to face Gavin fully. "If I'm very careful, and make sure to stay on the highest ground at the foot of the hill, maybe I could get around the flooded area. The road's paved after that, so…"

She was startled when Gavin took hold of her arm. Feeling the tingle where damp palm met damp skin, she swallowed. "Um…"

He gave a light tug. "Come over here a minute."

She allowed him to lead her off to the side of the property, a few yards to one side of the woods-lined drive. He motioned toward the river below them, at the bottom of a steep, muddy, rock-and-root-tangled incline. She remembered that the stairs down to the river lay at the back of the property. Only a few feet from the bottom of that staircase, a path led to the clearing in the woods where they'd sneaked away for a couple of sweet, private hours together the last time they'd been here.

She gazed down now with a sinking feeling in her

stomach and an old, dull ache in her heart. The sight below wasn't encouraging. Swollen by the storm, the river rushed and tumbled, carrying branches and other storm debris on its churning surface. "Maybe if I hurry, before the rain really starts falling again…"

"Sorry, Jen. That road's always dangerous when it's flooded. Dad and I talked about trying to get better drainage downhill, but the county hasn't been in any hurry to address the problem. If I thought I could drive that little car of yours safely through the flood zone, I'd have the guys follow me down and I'd do it for you. But even as long as I've been coming up here, I wouldn't risk your car or my life just to get you out a couple hours quicker."

A few more raindrops trickled down her face and she glanced toward the cabin. "Then I guess we should go inside before we get soaked again."

He released her arm, but didn't immediately move away from her. Instead, he raised his hand to wipe her cheek with his thumb, his gaze locked with hers. "So," he asked in a low, deep voice, "are you more anxious to run away from Avery or from me?"

She jerked away from his touch, then wished immediately that she'd been a little more discreet about it. "I'm not running away from either of you. I just… need to get out of this rain."

With that, she turned and moved briskly toward the cabin, resisting an impulse to run.

"Jenny…"

Pretending not to hear him, she walked a little faster.

It seemed her grandmother had been right about this trip to the cabin being a bad idea. But then, her grandmother claimed to be right about a lot of things. Gran had always said Gavin would break Jenny's heart. And now Gran claimed Thad and Jenny were the perfect match. She'd been right about the former. Maybe she was right about everything.

Jenny sat on the couch with a book she'd dug out of her bag, pretending to read in the glow of the fluorescent lantern next to her. She found the book dull as dishwater, but it was trendy among the social circles she and Thad moved in. It had been brought up during a dinner party last week, and she was the only woman there who couldn't intelligently discuss the book's theme. Thad had brushed off her chagrin later, telling her everyone should understand that her business kept her too busy for much reading time, but she'd made a mental note to try to stay more current. After all, there would be many more such gatherings in her future with Thad as he cultivated important connections among potential donors and supporters.

Being a political wife was a full-time job in itself, she'd murmured then with a nervous sigh. Thad hadn't disagreed, but he'd squeezed her hand and told her he had no doubt she would be as successful in a political partnership as she had been in everything else she'd tackled.

Not that everything she'd ever attempted had been a success, she mused, glancing up from the book to study Gavin across the cabin through her lashes.

She ran a fingertip absently along the page she was trying to read and chewed lightly on her lower lip. One of the reasons she'd needed this time to consider Thad's proposal was because she was so keenly aware of all the repercussions of accepting. How important it would be not to fail if she decided to take on the challenge. She wouldn't be simply formalizing a relationship, adjusting to day-to-day life with a partner who shared her bed and her breakfast table. Marrying Thad would change everything in the life she had worked very hard to achieve. And while she could certainly see the rewards, she was also aware of what she would be giving up. Her self-assigned task this weekend had been to weigh those pros and cons and decide once and for all which path was best for her, even though she'd been fairly confident her answer would be yes.

She closed the book. She would read it. Eventually. It was just too hard to concentrate with insufficient light and the distracting noise coming from the other side of the room. Frankly, she was more interested in the men's conversation.

Gavin and his friends sat around the table with beers and cards, playing poker while they waited for the rain to stop again. They had invited her to join them, but she'd declined. Aware that she was in the room, the men probably toned down the language a bit in their lively conversation. She'd smiled to herself when she heard a couple of quick substitutions for off-color adjectives. It didn't take her long to deduce that J.T. was also in law enforcement, though he was a state trooper rather than a city cop like Gavin and Avery. Their anecdotes, like their language, were probably toned down for her benefit, but still she winced a few times at the reminders of the unpleasant situations the three officers and the emergency medical technician found themselves in on a regular basis. She couldn't help thinking that this was a very different type of discussion than the ones

Thad and his friends engaged in. She wasn't judging, she assured herself, just noticing.

In addition to their work, they'd chatted about rowdy gatherings for barbecues and touch football games at various homes and parks, and about an upcoming charity baseball game between cops and firefighters that would apparently involve lots of beer and trash talk. They'd mentioned a patrolman who'd been hurt in a car crash during a high-speed pursuit, but was apparently recovering well. She bit her lip at the reminder that this cheerful, gregarious group willingly put their lives on the line every day in the course of their jobs. It was a brief glimpse of Gavin's life now—perhaps of the life she'd have shared with him had they stayed together. Lively, communal, but always with that underlying edge of worry.

She set the book aside and wandered to the window. The rain had almost stopped, though the gray sky looked more like dusk than midafternoon. She turned from the window to find Gavin watching her from the table.

"Do you need anything?" he asked. "Want me to put the kettle on?"

"Thanks, but I can do it." She forced a smile as she moved toward the stove. "I was just wondering how the road is looking down there."

J.T. looked up from the phone in his hand. "I just checked the weather radar. Looks like the rain's finally cleared. The flooding should start receding fairly quickly now. State and county police have been busy working wrecks all day, but it seems to be getting better out there."

"Considering everything, it's amazing we all have

the weekend off," Rob commented. "Can't even remember the last time that happened."

"So you decided to waste your day off cleaning up my property?" Gavin shook his head in skepticism.

Jenny saw his friends exchange quick glances, but Rob replied with a lazy chuckle and a shrug. "We owe you a few favors. Remember when you drove an hour and a half to help me out after that drunk ran a stop sign and hit my car in Brinkley? It wasn't raining, but it was cold. Below-freezing cold. We nearly froze our, uh, body parts off before we arranged to have my car towed and unloaded my things from it. All while you were facing the graveyard shift that night."

Gavin shifted uncomfortably in his chair. "That's not…"

"You sat up with me at the hospital for three nights straight when my dad was sick last year," J.T. joined in to add. "Brought me coffee and sandwiches, made calls for me, anything I needed. Mom was able to go home and get some rest because she knew you were keeping me company."

"Guys…"

Speaking over Gavin's embarrassed protest, Avery said flatly, "Truth is, we all owe you more than a few favors. Least we can do is to help you out here to keep you from doing any more damage to that shoulder."

Jenny wondered if most of that exchange had been for her benefit. Just what had Avery said to Rob and J.T. while she and Gavin had lingered for a few moments outside earlier? Had he told them that she and Gavin had once dated, that he believed she'd broken up with Gavin because she hadn't thought him good enough for her? Surely they didn't feel they needed to defend Gavin's character to her?

She gave Avery a narrowed look, but he merely gazed blandly back at her. Rob and J.T. weren't looking at her, but were smiling at Gavin. They seemed to enjoy their friend's discomfiture, as if good-natured ribbing was very much a part of their typical interactions.

Gavin tossed his cards on the table and scraped his chair against the floor as he pushed back. "Can't really focus on poker right now. I'm going to check those leaks in the bedroom again, make sure they aren't getting any worse."

"We can help with that, too," J.T. assured him. "Won't take long to nail down those shingles. That is, unless Avery tries to help. Boy's useless with a hammer," he added, making Avery grumble and the others laugh.

Biting her lip, Jenny filled the kettle. It was truly nice of Gavin's friends to have driven up to help him. Obviously they'd been worried about him up here, supposedly alone after a damaging storm, at risk for reinjuring himself with the repairs they knew he'd feel compelled to tackle. Perhaps they'd thought to cheer him up with their surprise visit, unaware that he had a visitor, even if an uninvited one. Very thoughtful and supportive of them, and yet…she could never have imagined she'd end up stranded here all day with Gavin and his buddies.

How much more bizarre could this weekend get? She wasn't having a bad time exactly, but it was just all so… awkward. And she still had to figure out a way to try to explain it all to her mother, her grandmother and Thad. They were certain to ask how her solitary weekend had gone, and she wouldn't lie to them.

"You want me to look at that wound for you?" Rob asked Gavin, who was pacing the living room and stretching his arm.

"No, that's okay. Jenny helped me change the bandage when it got wet earlier. It's fine."

She felt all eyes turn to her again, though she kept her attention focused on the selection of teas in the cupboard. She reached for the chamomile, deciding she needed its soothing benefits.

Avery stood, shifting his weight restlessly. "Did you lock the utility shed, Gav? The rain's done for now, I think. I can start hauling the ladder and extra shingles to the back porch so they'll be ready for us to use."

"I can help you with it."

"Rest your arm awhile. No need to overdo it."

"Avery's right," Rob agreed. "You've likely overused it already today. We're here now. Let us help."

"Look, I appreciate the offers, but…"

"C'mon, Gav, it's not every day you get offered free labor," J.T. chimed in with a laugh. "Most folks have to pay for repairs on their rental properties. All *you* had to do was get shot."

The box she'd just taken from the cupboard fell from Jenny's suddenly limp fingers, scattering tea bags over the countertop. The kettle whistled, but it took her a moment to remove it from the burner and turn off the gas. She felt as if she were trying to move through molasses as J.T.'s words reverberated in her mind.

Shot. Gavin had been shot? He'd lied to her?

She hadn't realized until that moment that after all these years, he still had the power to hurt her.

Chapter Four

J.T. seemed to sense immediately that he'd said something wrong. Maybe he picked up on the sudden tension radiating in waves through the room following his joking remark.

"I wasn't shot." Jenny sensed that Gavin directed the words to her, though he spoke to his friend.

Rob nodded. "Technically, that's true."

"Semantics," Avery pronounced with a wave of one hand. "I'd say being hit by shrapnel from a ricochet counts as being shot."

Gavin jerked his chin toward the back door in a less-than-subtle hint. "The utility shed is unlocked. The ladder's on the left and the spare bundle of shingles is on the shelf to the right."

"I'll help you carry the stuff, Avery," Rob offered, springing to his feet.

J.T. ambled toward the door behind them. "Might as well go out and take a look. We should be able to get started on the roof now that the rain's stopped."

"I'll be out in a couple minutes," Gavin said as his friends moved noisily outside.

Gavin waited only until the door had closed behind them before speaking to Jenny in a firm tone. "I wasn't shot."

She dunked her tea bag very deliberately into a mug of steaming water, her gaze focused fiercely on the task. "That's what you keep saying."

"I didn't lie to you, Jen."

He still read her all too easily. She moistened her lips. "Someone shot at you."

"I was responding to a domestic disturbance call. A guy high on meth was shooting wildly in a courtyard. I ducked behind an open door of a panel truck, he fired a few shots in my direction and some sharp pieces of metal from the truck embedded themselves in my shoulder. The wounds weren't life-threatening, but I had to have a minor surgical repair and I developed a mild infection afterward. Once the stitches come out in a few days, I'll do some physical therapy to loosen up the shoulder, and then I'll be back on the job. End of story."

She tossed the tea bag in the trash can. "Until the next time someone shoots at you."

"He wasn't shooting at me. Just firing in all directions. Like I said, he was high as a kite."

"Was anyone else hit?"

"No. The whole incident only lasted a few minutes. His weapon jammed and he was taken into custody. He's being held now for mental evals before standing trial."

She suppressed a shudder as she all too clearly envisioned the harrowing scene he'd described. "I guess I missed the news coverage."

How would she have reacted, she wondered, if she'd heard Gavin's name in a report of an officer shooting? It was one thing to hear about it when she could see him standing in front of her, looking relatively healthy and strong. But would she have panicked at not knowing how he was, even after all those years of not seeing him? Would she have hoped for the best and let it go, or would she have felt compelled to find out for certain that he would be okay?

He shrugged his good shoulder. "It happened the same day as that big warehouse fire downtown. The next morning there was that six-car wreck that shut down the river bridge and backed up rush-hour traffic for a couple hours. An addict with a gun in a high-crime neighborhood didn't make the lead coverage. Since I didn't actually take a bullet, the department downplayed the reports at my request."

"Just another day at the office," she murmured through a tight throat.

"Hardly. Despite what you see on TV, it's a very rare occasion when I have to draw my weapon, much less fire it. I was just standing in the wrong place at the wrong time that day. The only reason I didn't explain earlier was because I knew even after all these years, you'd turn it into an I-told-you-so."

She met his eyes fully then. "That was a rotten thing to say."

"Well?" he challenged, his brows drawn into a scowl. "Isn't that exactly what you're thinking? That you predicted ten years ago I'd probably get shot on the job?"

She hadn't predicted it exactly. But she had feared it with every fiber of her being. She saw no reason to point out that those fears had even more justification now. By how much had that shrapnel-scattering bullet missed burrowing into his chest? A few inches? Less? Would it have made the front page if the bullet had slammed into him rather than the truck door?

"You were willing to accept the danger."

"But you weren't."

Staring blindly into her tea, she heard a vague echo of her widowed mother's heartbroken sobs whispering in the back of her mind. Remembered her own grief at the untimely loss of her father. She had never wanted to risk that devastating loss again for herself. "Do we really want to have this discussion again?"

After a moment, he muttered, "No. Hell, no."

He moved toward the back door. "I'll go help the guys with the shingles. No need for you to come out this time. Enjoy your tea."

She had no intention of going back out unless her assistance was specifically requested. She very much needed some time alone, to regain her emotional equilibrium and steel herself against any further painful reminders of the past.

"Here, Gav, let me get that," Rob said as he reached for the good-size fallen limb Gavin had just picked up. "I'll haul it over to the burn pile for you."

"I've got it."

"It's a little heavy. Maybe I should…"

"I said, I've got it."

Rob held up both hands in response to Gavin's snap

and backed off deliberately. "Yeah, okay. It's cool. I'll just go get that one over there."

Gavin let out a gusty sigh and pushed a hand through his hair. Water was still everywhere, gathered in puddles, dripping from raised surfaces, running down every incline. The ground was a slick coat of mud over the rocky surface, making them have to plant their feet carefully. They hadn't yet started on the roof, but they'd been cleaning up debris. He'd been relieved that the damage was limited and easily repairable. It could have been much worse. Which didn't explain his lousy mood.

Avery stood nearby when Gavin turned from throwing the limb on the pile. Hands on his hips, he scowled at Gavin. "Damn it, you're letting her mess with your head again, aren't you?"

"I don't know what you're talking about."

"Right."

"She's not messing with my head."

"Then why'd you almost rip into Rob just because he offered to help you carry a branch?"

"Long day," Gavin muttered, a little embarrassed. "I'm tired. Shoulder's sore. And I'm hoping we don't find too much damage up on that roof."

Avery shook his head. "Yeah, that's a lot of excuses. And I'm not buying any of them."

"Okay, it's a little...weird that Jenny's here." He stumbled over the adjective, but he couldn't come up with a better one. "I wasn't prepared to see her, especially under these circumstances. It's not like I still have feelings for her or anything," he felt compelled to add. "It's just weird."

"Just don't forget how bad she—well, she and her

family—messed you up last time," Avery warned in a growl. "I'd sure hate to see that happen again."

"Not likely. Jenny's champing at the bit to get off this hill, and chances are I won't run into her again for another decade, if that."

"I notice you didn't say you're in a hurry to get rid of her."

Avery was concerned about him, Gavin reminded himself. And while the words annoyed him, he supposed the intention should count for something. "Why the hell do you think I've spent all morning trying to get that tree out of the drive?"

"Good," Avery said with a firm nod. "Because I doubt she's really changed all that much. Probably still a snob."

"Jenny wasn't a snob," Gavin said without stopping to consider. Her grandmother, on the other hand, was, though there was no need to get into that now. "We just had different goals in life. Being a cop's wife wasn't one of hers, for a lot of reasons."

His friend gave him a narrow-eyed scrutiny, as if trying to decide if he'd defended Jenny a bit too fervently. Gavin was relieved when J.T. called for his attention then. "Hey, Gav, I'm going up on the roof now. I forgot to ask where you keep the roofing nails."

"They're in a box on the shelf above the shingles," he called back.

"Didn't see them."

"I can't find them, either, Gav," Rob agreed from the open door of the utility shed.

"Hang on." With a glance at Avery's still-frowning face, Gavin moved away somewhat too eagerly.

He didn't want to talk about Jenny just then, neither

past, present nor future. Maybe because he was still trying to figure out his own convoluted feelings about all three. Maybe because he was starting to realize that after all these years he still wanted her. That he'd never really stopped wanting her.

Because the hammering from the roof was giving her a headache, Jenny moved out to the front porch. She wasn't sure what the guys were doing exactly, but it required lots of banging and a few shouts and a couple of trips in and out of the back bedroom, so she just got out of the way.

A cool, damp breeze brushed her face and toyed with the strands of hair on her cheek. The clouds were lifting, letting glimpses of sunlight glint among the rain-heavy leaves of surrounding trees. Emerging from their shelters, birds were starting to chirp again and a couple of squirrels played tag across the wet ground. If she ignored the sounds of the men in the backyard and on the roof, she could hear the river rushing past below the cabin.

This, she thought, was the scene she had envisioned when she'd booked the cabin. She'd pictured herself sitting on this porch rocker, perhaps watching a gentle rain fall around her—no stress, no interruptions, no reason at all to be "on" for anyone else's benefit. Away from her daily routines and obligations, she'd be able to reimagine her future, to see herself in a new reality. Once she returned to real life, rested and refreshed, she would be very busy planning a wedding, attending social and political functions, getting more acquainted with Thad's family and associates, business, personal and political. After the wedding, she and Thad would travel quite a bit, and when they were in town there would be functions nearly every evening.

She'd always wanted to travel, to see all the places she'd only read about. But she'd been so focused on establishing her business and planning for the second store, and others down the road, so careful with her budget, that she hadn't traveled nearly as much as she would have liked. All of that would change if—when— she married Thad. They would travel in style. Thad had even commented that she could take her mom and grandmother to some of the places they enjoyed exploring through television documentaries. Both women had worked so hard for so long, had seen so many of their dreams fall apart, it would mean a great deal to her to give them a few treats now.

It would be a good life. Comfortable. Secure. She would be able to use the skills she had developed in business and marketing, though perhaps not in the ways she'd expected. She'd be pushing Thad's objectives more than her own—though as he'd predicted, she would surely make them her goals, as well. She could still make her mark, just in different venues than she'd planned.

Thad promised to be a loyal and considerate partner. Their children would have all the advantages of a comfortable social position, he'd always said—the best education, exposure to the arts, chances to see other parts of the world. They would be raised with an awareness of the obligations of privilege, and with knowledge of the inner workings of government. Just as Thad himself had been raised, and look how well he'd turned out, he'd added with a charmingly self-deprecating chuckle.

Not once in the seven months she had dated him had

Jenny had to bandage Thad's injuries or pace the floor worrying about whether he would be shot on his job. Thad wasn't even a criminal lawyer. Unlike her fire-fighter father, whose favored off-duty pursuits were as risky—if not more dangerous—than his work, corporate attorney Thad could generally be found on the golf course when he wasn't helping some business VIP wade through legal paperwork. The odds were fairly good that Thad's daughter, if he should have one, would not be left fatherless at a young, particularly vulnerable age.

Maybe she'd finalized her decision, after all. With all the points she'd just enumerated, she would be foolish not to accept Thad's proposal. There were cons, of course, as there were to any decision, but the pros certainly outweighed them. There was no good reason at all for her not to marry Thad.

"Hey."

With a start, she turned to find Gavin watching her from the open doorway to the cabin. She had no idea how long he'd stood there. She'd been too lost in her thoughts to hear the door open. She cleared her throat. "Hey, yourself."

"We got the leaks fixed, I think."

She hadn't even noticed the hammering had stopped. "That's good. I hope there wasn't much damage."

"I don't think so, but I'll have someone out to check it before I rent the place again."

"Good idea."

"Look, I'm, uh, sorry about earlier. If I sounded…"

She shook her head quickly and cut in. "It's fine. Really."

His expression rather grim, he nodded. "The guys brought a big box of chocolate-chip cookies that J.T.'s wife made. They look really good. We thought you might like one."

"Thank you, but I'm not hungry."

"We're going down to check the road in a little while, after we take a short coffee break."

She sat up a bit straighter. "You think I'll be able to leave soon?"

"Maybe another hour or so, just to be sure."

She glanced at her watch. It was already four o'clock. It wouldn't yet be fully dark by five, so it should be safe for her to leave.

"You'll still have a long drive ahead of you back to Little Rock," he warned. "It will be late when you get back home."

"I could always stop somewhere along the way if I get tired. I'll be fine."

"You're in quite a hurry to get away, huh?" he said after a moment.

She shrugged, her eyes trained on her car in the driveway. "It seems best, considering everything. You've been a very gracious host and I appreciate it. But if I can get out safely today, I think I should go."

He didn't try to make another argument for her to stay. He would probably be relieved when she was gone, though she couldn't read any emotions in his expression.

"Go have your cookies and enjoy your company," she said. "I'll just sit out here and read awhile longer."

He hesitated only a moment, then nodded. "Let me know if you need anything."

"Thanks. I will."

He moved back into the cabin and closed the door quietly.

For the next fifteen minutes, she tried to read, but the

book still didn't hold her attention. Was she ever going to finish it? Did she really want to waste any more of her time with it? For all she knew, everyone's attention had already moved to another trendy title she would be expected to discuss.

She heard hearty male laughter coming from inside the cabin and she felt suddenly lonely. Maybe she'd go inside for a little while, after all.

"Hey, Jenny," Rob called out, looking up from his chair at the table when she walked in. He shook his shaggy dark hair out of his dark eyes and winked at her. "Come help me. I'm getting stomped over here."

She had assumed they were playing poker again, but she saw now that some sort of board game lay in front of them. Approaching them curiously, she laughed in surprise. "Scrabble? Really?"

"J.T.'s obsessed with the game," Rob answered with a gusty sigh. "He has to stay in practice because he and his wife bet household chores when they play each other."

"Hey, last time she beat me I had to cook dinner every night for two weeks," J.T. insisted with a laugh. "Well, every night I was home, anyway. I figure if I pick up some new words from you guys, I'll have an advantage next time I play her."

Sprawled in his chair, Gavin looked up from his rack of tiles. "I keep board games here for guests. J.T. dug this one out to play while we finish our coffee and cookies."

"Just don't tell anyone you caught us playing Scrabble and eating cookies instead of high-stakes poker with booze and cigars," Rob entreated comically.

"Your secret is safe with me." She was aware that Avery's laughter had faded when she'd entered the room, and he seemed to be making a point of not looking at her, but she wouldn't let him put her on the defensive again.

She circled round to stand behind Rob and look over the board and his rack. Some of the words on the grid made her raise an eyebrow. Her grandmother would certainly disapprove of a few. This explained some of the raucous laughter she'd heard.

With an exaggerated clearing of her throat, she reached out and rearranged a couple of Rob's tiles on his rack. He frowned at the board a moment, then laughed and slapped all of his tiles down in a triple-score play. "Boo-yah!" he crowed. "Top that, losers."

"Oh, that's no fair," J.T. protested with a shake of his head. "Jenny gave you the word."

"I'd have come up with it on my own. Probably."

"Right." Gavin's chair creaked as he shifted his weight. Though he was smiling lazily, he rested his right arm rather gingerly across his lap, and Jenny thought she saw a shadow of pain in his eyes. He had so overdone it that day, not that he had listened to anyone who tried to dissuade him, she thought in exasperation.

"Jenny's deadly at Scrabble," he drawled. "Dad thought he was the Scrabble champ until he took her on. The two of them got into some serious competitions. Holly called it full-contact Scrabble."

There was a barely notable moment of silence before Rob and J.T. responded with smiles. Jenny moistened her lips even as Gavin suddenly frowned, as if he'd become abruptly aware of just what he'd unthinkingly revealed about their past. It would be hard to maintain now that they had simply been passing acquaintances in college. Judging by the speculation on their faces, she realized that Avery must not have enlightened the others earlier, after all. She would leave it to Gavin to decide how much he wanted to tell them later, after she'd gone her own way again.

"Your dad was a worthy opponent," she said casually. "You were always pretty good yourself, but not your sister. Holly tended to make up words as she went."

"Yeah. Holly calls herself a 'cheerful cheat' when it comes to games."

She smiled. "I remember that."

Avery's chair scraped against the floor as he stood. "Let's go check that flooding down the road. Might need to shovel more brush and leaves out of the drainage ditches so Jenny can get out of here. And I've got to head back before long myself. Lynne and I are planning to stream a movie tonight."

She bit her lower lip. Avery was making no secret that he wanted her gone. Seriously, he acted as though she were a ticking time bomb or something. She couldn't imagine why she still roused such hostility in him after all these years.

The men were gone longer than she'd expected. After half an hour, she was beginning to worry that something had gone wrong. She sat on the porch for a while, then went inside and busied herself wiping the kitchen counters and cleaning the mud-tracked floor with a mop she found in the pantry. She preferred cleaning to sitting and waiting.

She had just put away the mop when she was startled by a burst of noise. Lights came on in the kitchen and the refrigerator began to hum, cooling the contents that would mostly have to be discarded. A ceiling fan in the living area began to spin lazily. Country music flowed from speakers she hadn't noticed before. Apparently Gavin's taste in music hadn't changed. Her heart clenched when she recognized the tune and the artist. But it wasn't "their" song, she realized after a moment, and thank goodness for that. It had been a long time after she and Gavin had broken up before she'd been able to listen to country music again, for fear that she might hear Diamond Rio's "Beautiful Mess," the song they'd both loved and which they'd always sung along to whenever it came on the radio in his truck.

She'd never been the type to have a little too much wine on a melancholy night, put on an old song and wallow in bittersweet memories. She started across the room with the intent to find the music player and silence it now. She liked this song just fine, though the sentiment about wanting a chance to spend one more day with a loved one made her a bit uncomfortable.

The front door opened before she'd taken more than a couple of steps. Looking as though he'd pretty much rolled in mud, Gavin entered alone.

She'd have thought the sight of him would have grown more familiar, that the impact of seeing him would have lessened. Yet, still her heart gave a hard thump when his eyes met and held hers across the room. She cleared her throat. "The power just came on," she said unnecessarily.

Gavin strode across the room and flipped a switch at the entertainment center. The music was abruptly silenced. Had he, too, been carried back to a more innocent time by the sound of a familiar voice? Or did he just want the music off?

"Where are the other guys?" she asked, her voice sounding loud in the sudden silence.

"They left. Avery wanted to get home, so I thanked them for their help and sent them on their way. All of them said for me to tell you goodbye and that they enjoyed meeting you today."

She doubted that Avery had sent quite those words, but she let it go. "How's the flooding?"

"It's going down fast," he assured her. "We dredged out the ditches again and pulled out some debris that was acting as a little dam. I'd give it another fifteen, twenty minutes, maybe, and then the road should be passable if you're careful."

A check of the time told her that in just over an hour, Thad would call. She'd like to be on the road by then. She could always pull over somewhere and take the call. She'd just rather not be here at the time.

Gavin pushed a hand through his hair. "I'm filthy. I'm going to try to scrape off some of this mud."

"Okay. I'll be carrying my things out to my car."

"Need any help with that?"

"No, thanks. I didn't bring in much last night."

He nodded, then disappeared into the back room. Moments later, she heard the shower running. She swallowed hard, deliberately cleared her mind of any unbidden images and started gathering her possessions.

His hair was still wet when he emerged again, but he wore a clean T-shirt and jeans and looked as though the shower had revived some of his energy.

"You didn't need help with the bandage?" she asked, glancing toward his covered shoulder.

He shook his head. "I managed. Thanks."

Lacing her hands, she glanced around the now cheerily lit room, trying to think of anything else to say. Coming up blank, she gave him a strained smile. "I guess I should try to make it out, then. Unless there's anything else I can do for you before I go?"

As she'd expected, he declined the offer. "No, it's all good."

She nodded. "Then I should go before it starts getting dark."

"I'll follow you down the hill in my truck, make sure you get across okay. I need to put my truck away for the night, anyway."

She'd be wasting her breath to tell him it wasn't necessary to see her off, so she merely nodded again. She took a step toward the door, then stopped when he moved to block her way. "What?"

His gaze was so intent on her face that she almost felt as though he could see her thoughts. "Just one more question before you go."

Suddenly nervous, she smoothed the hem of her shirt. "What is it?"

"Why did you really come here this weekend?"

She moistened her lips before answering. "I told you. I had work to do."

"Yeah, that's what you told me. And it's probably true. To an extent. But there's something more you haven't told me. Something that's been nagging at you. Probably none of my business, but you can always tell me to butt out, if you want."

"What makes you think I haven't told you everything?" she challenged, not quite meeting his eyes.

"Jen." He reached out and lifted her chin with a surprisingly gentle hand, so that their eyes met fully again. "I know it's been a decade since we've seen each other, but there was a time I knew you as well as I knew myself. There's a reason other than work that you came here, isn't there?"

She sighed. Perhaps it was the bittersweet reminder of their past that loosened her tongue. "The man I've been dating proposed to me last week. I came here to decide what my answer will be."

Chapter Five

She felt Gavin's hand twitch against her face, a spasmodic jerk he'd been unable to contain. And then he dropped his arm to his side, his thoughts now closed to her. She was sure her announcement had come as a surprise to him, but she couldn't tell how he felt beyond that.

"Well, isn't that a dilemma," he said. It wasn't quite a snarl.

Her chin rose. "It isn't an easy decision. Thad's a wonderful man, but I've worked hard to build the life I have now and obviously marriage would mean big changes for me. If you still know me so well, you should understand that I need to make sure I've considered all possible ramifications before I make a lifelong commitment."

"Sorry I got in your way this weekend. But I'm sure you'll make the decision that's right for you, anyway. You always have."

He opened the door and stepped outside before she could decide if she'd just been complimented or insulted. Wishing now that she'd kept her mouth shut, she swallowed a sigh and followed him outside.

"You have all your stuff?" he asked, pausing on the porch to don his mud-caked boots.

She nodded. "I think I have everything."

"I'll drive down ahead of you and make sure it's safe before you go through."

Though she thought he was being overcautious, she nodded. "Fine."

He climbed into his truck without another word. Apparently he wasn't going to say anything else about the admission she'd made to him. But wasn't he even going to say goodbye?

After a moment, she slid into her car. If he wanted to part with nothing more than a wave at the bottom of the hill, that was okay with her. It was probably even for the best.

He drove slowly down the hill and she followed at a safe distance. The road looked different in the afternoon light than it had in the darkness and rain on the way up. Much less forbidding and narrow, though the riverside fell away a bit more sharply than she'd have liked.

At the foot of the long hill, the road was still covered with a muddy puddle, but it looked no deeper now than it had when she'd driven through last night. Water rushed in the deep ditches along the roadside, and she saw the fresh trenches cut into the mud by the men's shovels. Gavin braked at the foot of the hill, then drove slowly through the puddle. As far as she could tell, he had no trouble getting to the slightly higher ground on the other side. He pulled over as far as he could on the

woods side of the road, hopped out of his truck and motioned for her to proceed. Following his example, she
drove slowly, staying in the center of the road. She heard
the water sloshing against the bottom of her car, but her
tires held their grip. Her enforced stay was at an end.

Gavin flagged her down when she'd reached the
other side. She put the car into Park as he approached.
So he was going to say goodbye, after all. She should
at least thank him for his hospitality before she drove
away.

Leaving the motor running, she opened her door and
climbed out. "That was definitely interesting," she said
with a wry smile.

"A little too interesting. If that puddle had been an
inch or two deeper, I'd have insisted you turn around
and drive back up the hill."

She was glad it hadn't come to that. "Well, it's been…"

She almost said "interesting" again, but decided
she was getting a little repetitive. She couldn't actually think of an appropriate adjective, so she allowed
her voice to fade into a wry smile.

"Yeah. It's been." He, too, left it at that. "Drive carefully."

"Thanks, I will."

"Again, sorry about the mix-up this weekend. I'll
make sure that refund goes through immediately. I assume it can just be credited back to your card?"

"Yes, that would be fine, thank you."

"I'll have someone other than Lizzie take care of it,
so it's done right."

She cleared her throat. "So…"

He met her eyes, though she still couldn't tell what
he was thinking or feeling. "So…"

"Goodbye, Gavin. Be careful with that shoulder, okay?" *And on the job*, she wanted to add. *Please don't get shot.*

"I'll take care," he replied without smiling.

She nodded and started to turn back to her car.

"Jenny…" His hand fell on her arm, detaining her before she could slide behind the wheel.

She glanced up at him. "Yes?"

She was too startled to move when he lowered his head and covered her mouth with his. Or at least that was what she told herself. She wasn't sure if she reached up to push him away or steady herself, but her fingers curled into his shirt.

His lips were as firm as they looked and so very warm. The kiss was brief, but it rocked her to her toes. Her heart pounded against her chest. She suddenly understood every old cliché about fireworks and trumpets.

During the past years, she had spent a great deal of effort trying not to remember explosive kisses and mind-blowing lovemaking with Gavin. On the rare occasion when erotic memories slipped through the cracks, she'd written them off as exaggerated by time, perhaps made more spectacular through the eager lens of youth and innocence. She'd convinced herself that no mere embrace could be that powerful now that she was a more experienced adult. No mere press of lips could turn her into a mindless mass of quivering nerves.

It seemed she'd been wrong. She couldn't for the life of her figure out why her eyes suddenly burned as if with long-held-back tears.

Oddly enough, Gavin was smiling a little when he lifted his head.

"Sorry," he said, though there was no apology in

his expression. "Guess you could say that was for old times' sake."

She realized that her hand rested just over his bandaged shoulder. She drew it away as if her fingertips had been burned. Her voice was hardly recognizable to her own ears when she said, "Goodbye, Gavin."

Only when she was in her car and driving away did it occur to her that he hadn't said goodbye in return.

At least their parting had been amicable this time, disturbing as the unexpected kiss had been. Maybe there'd been a little sarcasm on his part when she'd mentioned her potential engagement, but no anger, no accusations. Perhaps her chest ached a little, but that was probably a normal reaction. Gavin had been an important part of her past. Of course there would be some nostalgia, some vague reflections of what-might-have-been.

The weekend could not have turned out more differently than she'd expected, but maybe she'd accomplished what she'd set out to do, anyway. She'd said a final goodbye to her past. While sitting on the porch in the rocker, she had reminded herself of all she had to gain by marrying Thad. All in all, a surprisingly constructive day.

So why was there such a hard lump in her throat and a knot in her stomach? And why couldn't she stop reaching up to touch her lips, as if to see if they somehow felt different to her? And why was she finding it so hard not to compare that disturbing kiss to the pleasant, affectionate embraces she'd shared with Thad?

She had to stop. Going down that path could only lead to heartache again, surely, and she'd had enough of that to last a lifetime.

* * *

The dashboard clock said 5:59 when her cell phone buzzed half an hour after she'd driven away from the cabin. Knowing Thad, she figured her car clock was off rather than him.

She pulled into the parking lot of a closed tire dealership to take the call. She had to draw a deep breath before she answered with her usual measured tone. "Hello, Thad."

"Hi, sweetheart. How's the vacation?" His voice was rich and clear, mostly free of accent because he'd been raised to speak with a neutral Midwestern cadence rather than a Southern drawl.

"Over," she replied lightly. "You were right, it seems. The weather was just too unpleasant this weekend. I'm headed home."

"Are you all right?" She heard the concern in his voice. "You sound odd."

"I'm just a little tired. The storm kept me from sleeping well last night."

She would tell him about Gavin, she promised herself. Just not over the phone.

"I'm sorry to hear that. I hope you get more rest tonight."

"Thanks. How's your trip?"

"Successful." His tone was satisfied now. An image of him popped into her mind—gym-toned and slender, clad in pressed slacks and a discreetly expensive shirt, his chestnut-brown hair combed into his usual impeccably groomed style. If he'd been working in his room— as he almost always was when he wasn't out making valuable contacts—he was wearing the horn-rimmed glasses she teased made him look like a roguish professor. His handsome face would be creased with the indulgent smile he usually wore when he spoke with her.

Picturing Thad made her feel calm. Comfortable. Much preferable to jangled nerves and trembling fingers and knotted muscles, right?

They concluded their call with his usual breezy, "Love ya, Jenny," and her habitual, rather lame response of "You, too." The routine satisfied them both, so she saw no reason to change it.

She put her phone away and started her car again. She had quite a few more miles to travel that evening. She turned up the music—classical, not country—to distract her from the emotions that seethed inside her as she left the cabin and its owner behind her.

Gavin stood on the front porch of the cabin later that evening, studying the moon-washed grounds with weary satisfaction. The rain had stopped for good finally, and the clouds had parted. Tomorrow was supposed to be dry and sunny, which would let him put in another full day's work. He needed to stack and burn the remaining storm debris, and rake the lawn immediately around the cabin. The roof was repaired now, thanks to his friends, but he had a couple places to patch on the ceiling of the back bedroom. He had linens to launder, floors to clean and a couple of broken steps down toward the river to replace.

He was sore and bone-tired from all he'd done today. Every joint protested the very thought of all he planned to tackle tomorrow. But he was glad he had so much to do, mostly because the work would keep him too busy to brood about Jenny. Jenny, who was on the verge of marrying someone else, putting her out of Gavin's life again, this time forever. Jenny, whom he'd once planned to marry himself. He'd even fantasized about proposing here at the cabin, beside the river. Maybe in their private clearing, where he'd go down on one knee and offer her his paternal grandmother's ring. The pretty little diamond-and-sapphire band had been passed down to him when his grandmother died while he was still in high school. His grandfather had wanted him to have it to one day offer his own bride.

Maybe someday he'd pass it down to his eldest nephew. It seemed unlikely he'd ever use the ring himself, even if he found another woman he wanted to marry. In his mind, that ring would always have been meant for Jenny. Jenny, who hadn't wanted him, at least not without changing him into something he could never become.

Frowning in response to having her name pop up in his mind again—he'd lost count of how many times he'd had to push it away since she'd driven off—he spun on one heel and went back inside the cabin. It was time for his antibiotic, so he downed one with a glass of water. He flexed his shoulder tentatively, satisfied that it felt slightly less stiff, though still plenty sore. It would feel even better when he had the stitches out in a couple days. He was anxious to get back on the job and put this whole misadventure behind him.

The cabin seemed unusually quiet now that he was here alone. Usually he welcomed the tranquility. Tonight, though, the silence seemed almost oppressive. He thought about turning on music to listen to while he ate a can of chili he found in the pantry, but decided to dial in the television satellite instead. For some reason, country music didn't seem like a good choice tonight.

After eating, he cleaned the kitchen and carried the trash out to the plastic bin on the back porch. He opened the animal-proof lid, then froze when he saw the muddy, ruined green sneakers atop the other refuse.

He told himself to leave them alone, to bury them beneath the kitchen waste. Instead, he found himself cradling one of the small shoes in both hands, gazing down at it with a scowl. He'd promised to replace them, so it only made sense for him to check the size.

He was not prepared for the surge of hot blood that coursed straight to his groin. It wasn't the shoe that aroused him, but the wave of memories.

"Your toes are funny."

A girlish giggle, followed by "What's funny about my toes?"

"They're so tiny. You have teeny, tiny toes."

"I know. Stubby toes. I hate them."

"No. They're perfect. Funny, but perfect."

Naked and lazy, they had sprawled on a tumbled bed, bathed in candlelight. He'd proceeded to show her just how erotic funny little toes could be. And when her laughter had dissolved into low moans of need, he'd surged up her body to pay thorough homage to the rest of her.

Brought back to the present by the screech of an owl in search of dinner, he shifted his weight, preparing for a long, uncomfortably restless night ahead.

Something told him his dreams, if he slept, would be very disturbing that night.

Jenny opened her apartment door Sunday afternoon to find her friend Stevie standing on the other side, a bottle of wine in one hand, a familiar bakery box in the other. Her artificially blond hair brushed into a riot of curls, Stevie made a striking picture with her long-lashed, sapphire-blue eyes and generous, full-lipped mouth. She was the type of woman who turned heads wherever she went, a reaction she found more amusing than disconcerting. She was gregarious, energetic, generous to a fault and fiercely loyal. Jenny had several good friends, but Stevie was as close as she'd ever had to a sister.

"Moscato. Fruit tarts." Stevie held up each in turn. "I provide the treats, you spill the beans. I want to know everything about the night you just spent with Gavin Locke."

Though she rolled her eyes, Jenny motioned her friend into her living room. "I didn't spend the night with Gavin. Well, I did, but not… You know what I mean."

Stevie laughed musically and set the goodies on the kitchen bar. "I nearly dropped my phone when I saw your text saying Gavin was there at the cabin."

They'd talked briefly by phone earlier, so Stevie knew the basic details about how the mix-up had occurred, but she'd said she wanted the play-by-play in person. Truth be told, Jenny wasn't unhappy that her friend had come by. Sure, she could be tackling some of the paperwork she'd planned to complete that weekend, but it could wait. She reached into the cabinet for wineglasses. "You know where the plates are."

As at home in Jenny's place as she was in her own, Stevie was already serving the little tarts topped with glistening fruit. They carried the plates and glasses into the living room, where they kicked off their shoes and settled onto the couch.

"Have you told your mom and grandmother yet? About Gavin, I mean," Stevie asked, diving right into the conversation.

Jenny popped a glazed blueberry into her mouth, chewed and swallowed before she admitted, "No. They had a luncheon with their Sunday school class today. I didn't want to mention Gavin on the phone, so I just told them I came home early. I figured I'd tell them the whole story when I see them." Usually she had dinner with them on Sunday nights, but since they weren't expecting her to be in town this evening, they'd made plans with friends. She was seeing them tomorrow.

"Your grandmother's going to totally lose it when she hears Gavin's name," Stevie predicted with some relish. "Especially when she hears you spent a night with him."

"Stop saying that. We spent a night in the same cabin. We didn't spend the night together."

Stevie waved a hand. "Figure of speech."

"But an important distinction nonetheless." She certainly wasn't going to mention that she'd literally fallen into bed with Gavin when she'd arrived at the cabin.

"Maybe it would be easier if you don't tell them he was there."

Jenny shrugged in resignation. "Mom's going to ask about my weekend. She worried about me being there alone, and I know she'll ask how I weathered the storm. You know how she likes to hear all about my life. I don't want to lie to her. Even though they'll probably fuss, it just seems easier to tell them what happened. It wasn't my fault or Gavin's, so I'll just make it a funny-thing-happened story." At least, she would try to keep it that light and breezy, hoping to make it sound like no big deal that she'd run into him again.

"What was it like you when first saw him again? Did he look different? Does he look a lot older? Did he get, like, fat and bald?"

"He looks pretty much like he did, just a little older. More mature. Not fat. And he still has all his hair."

"He was always hot, in a sort of rough-cut way."

"You'd probably say the same about him now."

"Nice. So, he was surprised to see you, I guess?"

"Yes, he was. And he was embarrassed by his leasing company's error." She could so clearly picture him all tousled and grumpy and sleepy when she'd barged in on him. The image made her throat close. She set the plate aside and reached hastily for her wineglass.

"And you really had no idea he owns the place now?"

Stevie already knew the answer to that question, but Jenny shook her head and replied, anyway. "Of course not. I thought it was still just a vacation cabin, maybe owned now by the leasing company I contacted. I wasn't even entirely certain it was the one I'd visited before, though the photos and directions on the internet looked familiar."

"So Gavin didn't even cross your mind when you rented the place."

"Only in passing. I remembered what a good time I had with his family there. Maybe I wondered where he was these days, how he was doing—but I certainly never expected to get stuck in the cabin with him."

Stevie scrutinized a strawberry half. "So he's still single."

"Well, he's not married."

"Has he ever been?"

Jenny ran a fingertip around the rim of her glass. "I don't know. It didn't come up."

"So I guess you told him about Thad?"

"Yes, of course. As I was leaving," she added.

"As you were leaving? Seriously? What *did* you talk about until then?"

"Mostly about the storm and the damage it did. He told me a little of what's going on with his family. His sister has two little boys now, and I could tell he's crazy about them. Then his friends showed up and there wasn't a lot of time for personal talk. Um, Avery was with them. Did I mention that?"

"No, you just said some of his friends came to help clear the road." Stevie eyed her speculatively. "How's Avery?"

"He looks pretty much the same, too. Maybe his temples are a little higher, but he's still got red hair."

"How'd he act toward you?"

"Let's just say I'm still not his favorite person. He wasn't actively hostile…" Well, with the exception of the one low dig she saw no need to mention now. "But he wasn't overly friendly, either."

"He was always kind of a jerk."

Jenny bit her lip. She hadn't forgotten an unfortunate attempt at a double date when she and Gavin, who had been a new couple at the time, had invited their friends to join them in an unsuccessful bid at matchmaking. Avery and Stevie had not hit it off, to say the least. As she recalled, they'd argued about whether Nickelback "sucked"—Stevie liked their music; Avery hated it. A petty disagreement, but it had quickly escalated until they were hardly speaking by the end of the evening.

It was after that night when Avery had turned cool toward Jenny. She'd never known whether he'd blamed her for setting him up on an unsuccessful date, if he just didn't like her or maybe if he'd thought from the start that her relationship with Gavin had been ill-fated. Nor did she know why he disliked her now. Surely he didn't believe she still had any power to hurt Gavin.

"Had to be weird sleeping in the same house with Gavin again."

"I didn't sleep much," Jenny agreed, candid with Stevie in a way she didn't feel comfortable being with most other people. "Weird is pretty much an understatement for the way it felt to be there with him."

"I guess it brought back a lot of memories."

"Yes."

Stevie nodded thoughtfully. "It would be strange for me to spend the night with one of my exes. Though it's not like my past relationships were as epic as yours with Gavin. It took you a long time to get over him. For months you couldn't even talk about him. I can't imagine what it must have been like to suddenly be alone with him again."

Jenny squirmed a little on the couch and protested, "Come on, Stevie, there's no need to be so dramatic about it. It was a college romance, not a tragic love story. Yes, I was hurt when it ended, but obviously I got over it. I've dated since. Now I'm in a serious relationship with someone else. It's not as if I've spent the past ten years pining over Gavin."

"Hmph." Without pausing to expand on the enigmatic murmur, Stevie asked, "Did you tell Gavin you and I are still friends?"

"Your name came up. He asked if you were still dating the drummer."

"Who? Oh, him." Stevie laughed and shook her head. "I'd almost forgotten about him."

"Yeah, that's pretty much what I'd figured."

"Sticks was seriously cute. But sooo dumb."

"I remember."

Setting aside her plate, Stevie drew her bare feet beneath her and nestled back into the sofa with her wineglass cradled in her hands. "So what did Thad say? About Gavin being there, I mean. I assume you feel the need to tell him, too, since you're planning to tell the family."

Slowly swirling the liquid in her own glass, Jenny cleared her throat. "I haven't told him yet. I will, of course. It just wasn't the sort of thing to mention during a phone call. I figured I'd wait until he gets home so I can assure him face-to-face that it was all a perfectly innocent mix-up."

"Do you think he'll be mad?"

She chose her answering words carefully. "He won't like it, of course, but I doubt he'll be angry. Thad understands that mistakes happen. This particular mix-up was certainly awkward and unexpected, but he knows he can trust me. He'll be civil about it."

"Civil," Stevie murmured. "Yes, Thad is certainly civil."

Jenny frowned. "You make that sound like a criticism."

"Do I? Huh." Stevie sipped her wine, then asked, "So, I'm the only one you've told about your weekend adventure?"

Though she was tempted to press her friend to explain exactly why she was acting so oddly about Thad, Jenny decided to let it go. "I haven't really talked to anyone yet, other than you. Technically, I'm still on vacation."

"You are, aren't you? Want to go see a movie or something tonight? It's been forever since I've been to a movie. We'll find one with hunky guys who take off their shirts and blow things up—no sappy love stories."

Jenny set aside her glass. "I like the sound of that."

For one thing, there would be no need for conversation during a movie. Not to mention that she occasionally enjoyed watching hunky, shirtless men blow stuff up. Thad had never quite understood that, telling her it seemed out of character for her. The films weren't to his taste, but she'd told herself she was content to share those outings with Stevie while she and Thad confined their movie dates to more cerebral offerings. Most of which she also appreciated. She particularly enjoyed the lively discussions that followed over coffee or wine. It was just that every once in a while, she liked to turn off her brain and simply be entertained for a couple hours. And why not?

They decided to have dinner before the movie. They chose a popular, inexpensive Southwestern restaurant not far from the theater. Jenny kept an eye on the time, and she excused herself from the table they had just claimed when her phone buzzed quietly. She'd warned Stevie that Thad would call at six. Splashing hot sauce onto her burrito, Stevie waved her off good-naturedly, telling her there was no need to hurry with the call.

She took the call outside. It was hot and there was no shade from the still-blazing, early-evening sun, but these calls never lasted long. "Hi, Thad."

"I was beginning to wonder if you'd answer. Is everything all right?"

"Stevie and I are at a restaurant and I wanted to move outside to take the call."

"Oh, sorry. I didn't mean to interrupt your dinner."

"It's okay. We're just having burritos before we see a movie."

Thad's cultured laugh sounded quietly in her ear. "An adventure film, I'm sure."

She smiled. "Well, of course. It *is* Stevie."

A big "dually" pickup truck with chrome pipes and pounding bass passed in the parking lot. She waited until the noise had abated before asking politely, "What are your plans for the evening?"

"Another client meeting and then a dinner with some local associates. Oh, and I believe there's a celebrity on the guest list." He named several prominent national politicians, then an actor whose name she recognized immediately, which wasn't surprising. Thad was, after all, in LA representing one of his corporate clients.

"He's a friend of one of the senators," he explained. "I don't think I've seen any of his films, but I looked him up online so I won't sound completely disconnected from popular entertainment."

"You should have asked me," she quipped. "I think I've seen all his movies."

"Of course you have." He laughed again. "Once you start attending all these events with me, I'll depend on you to keep me up-to-date. I know you'll want to continue to make time for your girls' nights with Stevie because you enjoy her company so much, so I'll shamelessly pump you for details about the action films I miss."

He was obviously taking for granted that her answer to his pending proposal would be yes. And why shouldn't he be? They were obviously a well-suited couple; even the activities they didn't share in common complemented each other. It went without saying that it might be harder to make time for these girls' nights after the wedding, but Thad was making it clear he'd never deliberately interfere with the longtime friendship.

Theirs wasn't, perhaps, an "epic love affair," to use Stevie's words. But she and Thad were comfortable together. She could make that be enough.

Two squealing adolescents streaked down the sidewalk, shoving their way past her with insincerely muttered apologies. An ambulance shrieked by on the street, the decibel level making her wince. The parking lot smelled of exhaust, warm asphalt and fried foods. She pictured Thad in his five-star hotel surrounded by quiet elegance, and then imagined herself there beside him, choosing jewelry to enhance a little black dress rather than the cool cotton top and cropped pants she wore now.

Roused from her mental drifting, she blinked when he spoke again. "I'll let you get back to Stevie. Have fun. Love ya, Jenny."

"You, too." She lowered her phone to her side, stood for a moment staring at the traffic moving in front of her, then turned abruptly to go back inside.

"I'm sorry," she said, sliding into her seat across the little plastic table from Stevie. "I'm muting my phone for the rest of our evening. Anyone who needs me can leave a voice message or send me a text."

Stevie sipped from a straw, then set the paper cup of soda aside. "How's Thad?"

Stevie used almost exactly the same tone whenever she spoke of Thad. Always polite, not quite cool but not really warm, either. Perhaps that warmth would come with time. But even if Stevie and Thad were never close, their careful courtesy was certainly better than the resentment Avery had always exhibited toward herself when she'd dated Gavin.

"Thad's fine. He's having dinner with a few names you'd know tonight." She listed the ones she remembered, including the actor, and watched Stevie nod in recognition.

"Cool. So, Thad's really working the political connections, huh?"

"He's certainly drawn in that direction."

"Does it bother him that you've never been all that interested in politics?"

"I've always been active in the community," Jenny countered quickly. "You know how many organizations I've been involved with. Not political exactly, but civic-minded. I like the idea of helping Thad make a difference with whatever talents I have to contribute."

"Mmm."

Jenny figured if Stevie bit her lip any harder, it would start to bleed. She focused on her meal and changed the subject. "How's your burrito?"

"It's good. So, Gavin's still a cop, huh? I guess it's worked out well for him."

"Gavin was at the cabin to recuperate from being shot in the shoulder," Jenny said bluntly, if not entirely accurately. "If you call that working out…"

Stevie flinched dramatically. She knew all too well the fears that had come between Jenny and Gavin all those years ago. "Oh, crap. You didn't mention that. Is he okay?"

"He's fine. I heard him tell his buddies that he was eager to get back to work."

She changed the subject abruptly, and Stevie got the message that talk of Gavin was over for the evening.

Yet Jenny couldn't help but remember the determination in Gavin's expression when he'd assured his friends he would be back in uniform the minute he was cleared for duty. And they'd all cheered him on, damn it. Had she been the only one who worried that he wouldn't be so lucky next time?

Chapter Six

"I can't imagine what it must have been like to be stranded in a mountain cabin with an ex-boyfriend." Tess Miller stared wide-eyed across the restaurant lunch table at Jenny the following Thursday, shaking her auburn head in dismay. "If that had been me with my ex, there might have been bloodshed before morning."

"Now that's a story that sounds interesting," Stevie commented with a lifted eyebrow.

Tess laughed and shook her head. "It would take a great deal of wine and longer than any of us have for a lunch break."

Tess had called earlier that morning to say she was going to be running a business errand near Complements at lunchtime and to ask if Jenny and Stevie, both of whom she had met in a yoga class, would be free to join her. Stevie worked as a freelance interior designer specializing in kitchen remodels, and she'd happened to have a couple spare hours that afternoon to meet them at a favorite restaurant in the same shopping center as Jenny's store.

"Maybe we should have another girls' night soon," Stevie suggested, scooping rice onto her chopsticks. "I haven't spent nearly enough time with my girlfriends lately. I really should spend more time doing things I want to do, rather than… Well, anyway."

Which only confirmed to Jenny that Stevie's relationship with Joe, the bass player, wasn't going all that well, though Stevie hadn't yet admitted it. Even to herself, perhaps?

Tess sighed. "I have plenty of free nights to hang out when I'm not working, considering that my experiment in online dating has been pretty much a bust so far."

Jenny grimaced. "The latest one didn't work out?"

"Let's just say he sent me some photos of himself. I have now blocked all future communications from Captain Underpants."

Stevie laughed. "Captain Underpants? Oh, I *definitely* have to hear this story."

Tess shuddered delicately. "It's going to take more than wine for that."

All three laughed.

"Did you ever find the nerve to tell your mom and grandmother who you found in the cabin, Jenny?" Stevie asked.

Groaning, Jenny nodded. "Yes. It was…uncomfortable." She was wildly understating that exchange and Stevie probably knew it. Her grandmother had been horrified.

"Nothing happened, Gran," Jenny had assured her firmly. "Gavin was a perfect gentleman. We slept in different rooms. Considering the damage done by the storm, I'd have been in more trouble if he hadn't been there. I'd have been stranded up there alone."

Pointing a fork at Jenny over the dinner table Monday night, Gran had grumbled, "That's exactly why I said it was foolish of you to go there alone in the first place. I could understand if you'd wanted to visit a nice spa, or fly to New York to shop and see shows, or some other civilized vacation. But to make a three-hour drive by yourself to some backwoods fishing cabin made no sense to me at all."

Jenny's mom had tried to defend her. "She just wanted some quiet time to work and to think, Mother."

"She lives alone," Gran had pointed out acerbically. "All she had to do was turn off her phone and lock her door."

"I wanted to get away from the sounds of traffic and sirens for a few days. Maybe walk alongside the river and listen to birds sing. That's not really so strange, is it?" Jenny had tried not to sound defensive, but wasn't sure she'd been successful.

"Hmph. I can't help wondering if you knew that man would be there," Gran had muttered darkly. "He always had a strong hold on you. Seems like a strange coincidence that the minute your nice, ideal boyfriend is out of town, you run off to a cabin that just happens to be owned by that…that cop." She spat the word as if it were a synonym for *criminal*.

Jenny had to bite her tongue to keep herself from snapping at her grandmother, though she had spoken acerbically. "I don't appreciate your implication that I would sneak around and lie to either you or Thad. If

I had chosen to meet Gavin—or anyone else, for that matter—at the cabin, I'd have made no secret of it."

"How was Gavin?" her mother had interceded, just a hint of wistfulness in her tone. "He was such a sweet boy. And his mother was a nice lady. Did he say how she is?"

Before she could reply, her grandmother had interrupted. "For heaven's sake, Brenda, what do you care about that man's family?" Gran had demanded with a scowl. "You should be more interested in *Thad's* lovely mother. Have you heard from her since he's been out of town, Jenny? You have spoken with Thad, haven't you?"

"I talk with Thad every evening," she'd answered with every ounce of patience she'd possessed. "His parents are on a Mediterranean cruise to celebrate their fortieth anniversary."

"A Mediterranean cruise." Lena Patterson's eyes had gleamed with envy. "I'd always hoped to take a cruise with your grandfather, bless his soul. We'd have had a nice life like that, had he lived."

Gran made no secret of her lifelong sorrow that her young physician husband had died of an unforeseen, massive heart attack at the age of twenty-nine. He'd died just before he'd paid off the last of his education loans, before he'd been able to set up his practice and provide her the life of a respected doctor's wife she'd fantasized about. Gran had worked long hours to help put him through medical school, along with the loans they'd taken out, and she believed now that her efforts had gone unrewarded. She'd been left a pregnant widow with no one to support her except herself. Not at all the life she'd planned.

Still, Lena had always been a resourceful woman.

She'd served as the secretary to the president of a medical supplies company, working up to a good salary and a tidy pension there. After paying off her late husband's loans, she had invested the small life-insurance settlement from him and a modest inheritance from her own parents into rental property. For nearly forty years, while still working full-time, Gran had been a landlady. A shrewd one, at that, providing a good life for herself and her daughter. She'd sold her last property a few years ago, for enough to supplement her pension and Social Security quite comfortably. She had never remarried, which always made Jenny wonder if Gran had truly loved her husband for more than his potential earnings.

Gran had been bitterly disappointed when her daughter had also become a debt-ridden, widowed single mother after marrying beneath her, in Gran's opinion. Gran had been determined the pattern would end with her granddaughter.

Gran saw Thad as embodying everything she had wanted for herself, whereas Gavin had seemed to represent all the heartache and regret she and her daughter had suffered. Gran had insisted that she didn't want her granddaughter to marry only for money; but she'd often quoted the old adage that it was just as easy to fall in love with a rich man as a poor one.

Jenny realized suddenly that Tess and Stevie were studying her across the table with mirroring looks of concern. She blinked. "What?"

"You kind of zoned out there for a minute," Tess replied quietly.

Jenny sighed and shook her head. "I'm fine. Let's

just enjoy our lunch, okay? I have a meeting with a supplier later this afternoon, and I need to prepare for it."

Stevie started to speak, then stared over Jenny's shoulder toward the entrance door with widened blue eyes. "Oh, my gosh, is that…? Yes, I think it is. Wow."

Jenny looked up from her lunch to study her friend's face curiously. "Someone you know?"

"Someone *you* know," Stevie murmured. "And let's just say, time has been very good to him."

Jenny set down her chopsticks. The tiny hairs on her arms were suddenly standing on end. She didn't have to ask her friend for further clarification. If she were a superstitious woman, she'd wonder if she had somehow summoned Gavin with her wandering thoughts.

Jenny couldn't blame either of her friends for staring when Gavin stopped at their table. He was the type of man who elicited such a reaction. Heightened senses. Accelerated heartbeat. Visceral feminine awareness. It was the way she had responded to him the first time she'd noticed him in a college classroom. She reacted the same way now.

He was dressed in dark jeans and a short-sleeved navy pullover almost the same color as his eyes. The casual clothing emphasized his broad shoulders, strong arms and solid thighs. He hadn't cut his hair yet. It waved back from his clean-shaven face as if he'd just run his fingers through it, the lighter streaks gleaming in the dark blond depths. She doubted that he'd deliberately tried to look like a walking sexy-bad-boy poster—he'd be appalled at the very suggestion—but he did, anyway. And judging by the admiring looks from women at nearby tables, she and her friends weren't the only ones who noticed.

"Hello, Gavin," she said when he didn't immediately speak. She took some pride in hearing the evenness of her tone; she doubted that anyone who heard her could tell how rapidly her heart was racing. "Were you looking for me or is this another crazy coincidence?"

"The manager at your store told me I could find you here." He set a bag from a nearby shoe store on the table next to her plate. Her left hand rested there and he brushed her bare ring finger with his fingertips as he released the bag. Was that merely an accident?

"I figured since you were close by, I'd deliver this to you personally," he said, his voice a shade deeper than usual.

"What…?". She glanced into the bag, then shook her head when she saw the familiar shoebox. According to the label, this was an identical pair of shoes to the ones she'd ruined at the cabin, right down to the neon-green color. They were not inexpensive shoes. Even though he'd told her he would, she hadn't really expected him to replace them, especially not in person. "You didn't have to buy me new shoes."

He shrugged. "It was the least I could do after you helped me clean up the storm damage. Did the new leasing agent refund your credit card?"

"Yes, thank you. Did you fire Lizzie?"

"Wasn't my call to make, though I did file a complaint with the company. I understand she quit Monday afternoon. She didn't care for the job apparently." He turned his head to nod to her companions. "Ladies."

Remembering her manners, she said quickly, "Oh,

sorry. Gavin, this is my friend Tess Miller. And you remember Stevie McLane?"

"Of course he does." Stevie hopped from her chair to give Gavin a typical Southern greeting of a quick hug. "Gavin, you look great. You've hardly changed. I knew you right away."

He gazed down at her when she stepped back. "Were you this blonde in college?"

She giggled. "Why, of course I was."

Though they all knew she wasn't fooling him in the least, he merely chuckled. "Well, it works for you. You look good."

Stevie batted her lashes. "Thank you, sir."

Jenny remembered that Gavin and Stevie had flirted teasingly in college—all in good fun, neither of them taking it seriously. She'd never felt even a twinge of jealousy toward them then. She told herself it didn't bother her now that he was smiling down at her friend, looking relaxed as he hadn't been with her.

Tess was eyeing Gavin with a slight frown. "I think we've met before. Aren't you the officer who responded to a break-in at my office a couple of months ago? Prince Construction Company?"

"Yes, I thought you looked familiar. Your boss's office was ransacked, but nothing taken that you could see, right?"

She nodded. "We finally decided it was someone looking for quick cash. And since we don't keep cash at the office, they were out of luck."

"It's nice to see you again under more pleasant circumstances."

"You, too, Officer Locke."

"Call me Gavin."

"This is quite a coincidence. That you've met before, I mean," Stevie said, looking from Gavin to Tess.

Gavin's eyes turned to Jenny as he murmured, "There've been quite a few of those lately."

Stevie made a sound as if she'd suddenly had a brilliant idea. Because she'd seen so many of Stevie's brilliant ideas go terribly wrong, Jenny tensed as Stevie tugged at Gavin's arm and burst into excited speech.

"My boyfriend's band is playing on the deck at Benoit's Pier Saturday night. Very informal, and it's an over-twenty-one-only crowd, so we don't have to deal with teens and frat boys. It's a twenty-dollar cover charge to pay the band and to keep out the troublemakers. There's going to be a donation box to raise money for the victims of the spring storms that have hit Arkansas this year, but it's a no-pressure fund-raiser. You could even bring one or two of your buddies if they'd like to come hear some great music and meet new people. Or, um, bring a girlfriend if you have one."

Jenny had to stop herself from openly grimacing. It seemed she'd been right to worry. What was Stevie thinking?

Gavin smiled at Stevie as if her wording had amused him. "No girlfriend at the moment."

"All the more reason for you to come, then." She patted his arm lightly. "Lots of hot single women will be there. Tess, here, for example."

Tess choked on a sip of tea. "Stevie!"

Stevie gave her a blandly sweet smile. "Just saying." She gazed back up at Gavin. "Well? Are you interested?"

He shrugged the shoulder Jenny knew to be uninjured while she held her breath waiting for his reply. He would say no, wouldn't he? Surely he would say no.

"Maybe," he said instead, making her fingers curl tightly in her lap. She wasn't sure who she most wanted to strangle, him or Stevie. Gavin glanced her way before asking, "Are you all going to be there?"

"Yes, we are," Stevie answered cheerily. "Tess and Jen have already promised they'd be there to keep me company while my boyfriend is playing. My friends always keep their promises."

Jenny glanced at her friend and resisted the urge to shove the napkin in her mouth.

"So, we'll see you Saturday?" Stevie prodded Gavin.

"Sure. Why not?" He winked at Jenny and her heart clenched. "See you."

He turned and strode out of the restaurant in a rolling gait that was undeniably sexy. Jenny was well aware that she was only one of many appreciative women studying his very fine backside as he left. Damn it.

Dragging her eyes away, she whirled on Stevie, who was settling back into her seat with an exaggeratedly innocent expression. "What the hell was that?"

"What?"

"Why did you invite Gavin for Saturday night?"

"Just an impulse. Why not invite him? Maybe he'll bring some cute cop friends."

Jenny asked pointedly, "Aren't you going to be there with Joe? You know, your current boyfriend?"

Stevie waved a hand. "I am. But Tess, here, is looking. And I have other single friends who'll thank me for inviting Gavin. Sandy, for example. You know she has a thing for men in uniform."

"Sandy has a thing for men. Period." She could only

imagine how Sandy would react to seeing Gavin among the usual crowd. Like a hungry hawk spotting a particularly tasty prey, most likely. The image made her stomach tighten, but only because she'd hate to see any of her male acquaintances caught up in Sandy's avaricious talons, she assured herself.

Stevie giggled. "True. But there's still Tess. You thought Gavin was good-looking, right, Tess?"

"I have eyes," Tess said drily. "But I also have a rule against dating friends' exes. That never works out well for the friendship."

This was Jenny's cue to assure Tess that she had no objections at all if Tess and Gavin were to hook up at the party. But she toyed with the remains of her lunch and said nothing.

"Besides," Tess said speculatively, "it seemed to me as though Gavin is still interested in Jenny. You saw the way he looked at her, right?"

Jenny reached hastily for her water glass and took a deep sip before saying, "You're wrong about that. He's aware that I'm seeing someone else. But even if I weren't, trust me, Gavin is no more interested in getting involved with me again than I am with him. That ship sailed—and sank—a long time ago."

"So you'd be fine with him dating Tess, or anyone else he might meet at the party?"

Shooting Stevie an irritated look, Jenny muttered, "Of course."

She pushed her plate away then. "I really should get back to the store. I have a ton of things to do today."

Stevie reached out quickly to touch her hand. "Sorry, Jen. Don't rush off. I'm just teasing you."

"Yes, I know. It's just a busy day for me."

Her teasing amusement gone now, Stevie looked anxious. "You didn't really mind that I invited Gavin, did you? You said the two of you got along fine at the cabin, so I figured it was okay to invite him and maybe some of his friends. For the band and the fund-raiser's sake, of course."

"No," Jenny lied evenly. "Of course I don't mind. It just surprised me, that's all."

Maybe she'd come up with a reasonable excuse so she wouldn't have to attend. It wasn't her type of gathering, anyway. She was only going because Stevie had wheedled a promise out of her, saying she needed someone to talk to while Joe was playing. Since Thad was out of town, anyway, it wasn't as if Jenny had anything better to do. Now if only there were some honorable way to get out of that promise...

"You did tell Gavin that you're seriously involved with Thad, didn't you, Jenny?" Tess asked curiously. "I mean, the way he looked at you, I'm not sure he understands you're fully off the market. And he bought you shoes."

Snatching up her purse and the shopping bag, Jenny stood. "I really do have to go. I'll pay at the register on my way out. I'll talk to you both later, okay?"

Her friends probably watched her hasty departure with open mouths of surprise. They would certainly be unable to resist speculating about why she'd felt the need to bolt. But she had a sudden, almost desperate need to find someplace quiet where she could just be alone to think.

She was well aware of the irony that it was the same aspiration that had gotten her into this mess in the first place.

* * *

After mentally debating for a couple of days about whether he would attend, and then going back and forth on whether to ask one or more of his friends to come along, Gavin showed up at the Saturday-night event alone. Even as he'd made the drive to the venue, he'd almost turned around a couple of times and headed back home, asking himself why he was doing this. He wasn't a party guy, and he wouldn't know anyone here other than Stevie and Tess…and Jenny, of course. His suspicion that spending more time with Jenny was his primary motivation for going almost made him change his mind again.

He'd thought of asking Avery, but since Avery and Jenny didn't get along—not to mention the bad history between Avery and Stevie—that hadn't seemed like a great idea. So he'd come stag. He had nothing better to do that evening, anyway, as it would be another week before he was cleared for duty again. The fund-raiser seemed like a worthy cause, though he wondered if it was simply an excuse for a party. And yes, maybe he wanted to see Jenny again, if only because he'd been wryly amused by the expression on her face when Stevie invited him.

It wasn't that he expected anything to happen between them, he assured himself. After all, she was seeing another guy. She was considering getting engaged, if she hadn't already. Yet, he'd noted the lack of a ring on her finger, which could mean she hadn't yet made that leap. She certainly hadn't seemed all that sure about it when she'd broken the news to him. If she wanted to marry the other man, wouldn't she have jumped on the chance to accept his proposal? If she really loved the guy, would she need to go off by herself to "consider all possible ramifications" before giving her answer?

None of those things were any of his business, of course. If Jenny wanted a practical, socially advantageous marriage which probably had her snobby grandmother salivating in delight, then it was entirely her choice. Hell, maybe she'd even be happy in such a union. But if she really loved that Thad guy, would her skin have flushed, her eyes dilated, her heart have pounded in her throat when Gavin had impulsively kissed her? He'd looked at her closely when he'd drawn reluctantly away, and he'd seen every one of those reactions. Had her response to him been due to nothing more than surprise? Had he only imagined that the sizzling attraction between them had flared back to life the moment she'd stumbled into his bedroom? Did those old feelings still burn only in him?

Maybe he just needed to make one last attempt at finding out for certain before he closed the door on their past again, this time for good. He wasn't one to encroach on another man's claim, but the last he'd heard, Jenny hadn't given an answer yet. It wasn't a done deal until she made that pledge, right?

Maybe he'd meet the guy tonight, and see for himself that Jenny was happy. Wasn't that all he'd ever wanted for her? For himself?

The band was playing on the open-sided, covered deck of a Little Rock restaurant and club located on the bank of the Arkansas River. The sun had just set when he arrived. The big deck glowed with gold fairy lights hanging from overhead and strung in numerous potted trees. Soft floodlights were tucked discreetly into corners. A dais was set up for the band with the river view behind them, but as he paid his cover, he was informed by the hostess that the band was on a short break. Recorded music played from speakers until they took their places again.

He scanned the milling crowd for familiar faces. Surprisingly, he spotted a few, though they weren't people he knew personally. Quite a few were young movers and shakers not yet in the upper ranks but on track to get there. People who didn't blink at spending twenty bucks just to get into a club, not to mention whatever they'd stuff into the donation box or spend on drinks. As for himself, this was a fairly expensive evening.

Tables of nibbly-type food flanked the sides of the deck, and drinks were served at a cash bar by white-coated bartenders. The chatter and laughter was lively and animated, but acceptably modulated. This was not one of the clubs to which he and his associates in uniform were regularly summoned for disturbance calls.

He glanced automatically down at his clothes. He'd opted for khakis, a dark green polo shirt and brown slip-ons. He'd even had a haircut. Outwardly, he supposed he blended in fine with the other men in attendance, many of whom wore similar attire, but he still felt like the outsider for some reason. He had to admit he'd be more comfortable in a sharply pressed uniform with his sidearm at his hip.

"Hello." A busty brunette in a fluttery top and tight miniskirt approached him, making him wonder how she could walk at all in heels so high they practically put her feet at a vertical angle. She looked good, he had to give her that, but his tastes ran toward a more subtle beauty. "I'm Sandy. Are you looking for someone in particular?"

He smiled. "Hi, Sandy, I'm Gavin. And I'm trying to find Jenny Baer or Stevie McLane. Do you know them?"

She ran a hand over her hair, a gesture perhaps intended to hide her disappointment with his answer. "As a matter of fact, I do. I just saw them by the railing looking over the river. Behind that big ficus tree with the little gold lights in it?"

"I'll find them, thanks."

"Catch you later, maybe?"

He nodded. "Sure."

Threading through chatting guests, he made his way to the railing. Stevie had her back to him, but he recognized her immediately. Her bright blond curls gleamed in the yellow lights from the potted ficus. She stood next to a tall, lanky man. Despite the warmth of the evening, he wore a wrinkled, long-sleeve, black-and-green plaid shirt over a white tee, black pants turned into cuffs at the hems and scarred brown work boots. A misshapen gray porkpie hat with a plaid band and a stupid little feather sat on top of his floppy hair, and he'd finished the look with horn-rimmed glasses and sideburns that covered his jaws almost to his chin.

Gavin almost groaned. Seriously? This dated hipster poser was Stevie's latest? She might have done better to have stuck with the grunge drummer from college.

The poser shifted his weight and someone else came into view. Gavin swallowed. Here was the reason he'd cut his hair, ironed his khakis, shelled out twenty bucks and risked embarrassment to come to this gathering that was so far from his comfort zone.

Jenny looked cool and lovely in a sleeveless white scoop-necked summer dress that hugged her bust and flared out from her hips to just above her knees. Her dark hair was loose in soft layers around her pretty face and fell just to her bare shoulders. He noticed a touch of glitter on her eyelids and peach gloss on her full lips. His gaze lingered on those lips that he'd tasted so recently and which he suddenly hungered to sample again.

You are such an idiot, Locke.

Would he really even think about putting himself through it all again, even if she were willing to try? He recalled everything they'd been through, all the obstacles that had stood between them back then and hadn't really changed since, all the pain he'd endured, the ache of missing her that had tormented him for a long time after he'd walked away from her. Was there any chance in hell that anything would turn out differently if she'd be willing to dump Prince Charming to give it another shot?

And still he wanted her. Had never really stopped wanting her.

Idiot indeed.

She'd been talking to someone when he'd approached. Tess, he realized, dragging his gaze away only long enough to identify the other woman and then feeling his eyes drawn inexorably back to Jenny.

He'd tried to love other women in the years since they'd split. He'd made a concerted effort to move on, focusing on his training, his job, his friends and a procession of women as different from Jenny as possible. He'd even considered one relationship fairly serious. It had never gotten as far as an engagement, but they'd flirted with the idea, until they had decided by mutual agreement that, while they'd had fun, they weren't meant to spend a lifetime together. The night he and

Blair had called it quits, he'd sat alone in his darkened apartment until dawn, drinking and thinking not of Blair, but of Jenny. And that had been several years after he'd last seen her, leaving him to ask himself despairingly if he was destined to end up a grumpy old bachelor cop, haunted by memories of the one who'd got away.

And here she was again. Tying him in knots just like before. And no matter what happened from here, seeing her again had already put her firmly back into his... his mind, he substituted quickly, refusing to acknowledge the word that had almost formed in his thoughts.

She glanced his way, then froze momentarily. For one unguarded moment, he saw the reaction in her eyes. A flood of emotions he couldn't quite decipher, but that he couldn't mistake. And then she seemed to gather herself, hiding those feelings behind a placid expression and a polite smile. "Hello, Gavin."

He returned the greeting and moved closer to her, nodding to the others as he did so.

Pivoting fast enough to make the fancy drink in her hand slosh against the sides of the glass, Stevie smiled brightly at him. "Gavin, I'm so glad you could come. Joe, this is Gavin Locke, the friend of Jenny's I told you about. Gavin, this is Joe Couch, the bass player for Eleven Twenty-Five."

Joe switched his beer mug to his left hand so he could stick out the right toward Gavin. "Hey."

"Eleven Twenty-Five?" Gavin asked, briefly shaking the other man's hand.

"My band. We're about to start playing again." Joe eyed Gavin somewhat warily through lenses Gavin cynically suspected to be clear glass. "So Stevie says you're like a cop or something?"

"LRPD," he confirmed.

"Uh. That's cool, I guess."

Gavin got the distinct impression that Joe was not a fan of police. Probably believed all the bad stories he heard and ignored the good ones. Gavin was all too familiar with the type. He had no intention of defending the integrity of law enforcement officers to this guy, though, so he merely turned back to Jenny. He nodded toward her empty hands, then glanced at Tess, whose hands were also free. "You two aren't having anything to drink?"

"Tess and I just got here," Jenny replied lightly. "I'll probably have a glass of wine in a few."

"And I'm the driver, so I'll stick to strawberry lemonade," Tess added. "They mix a really good one here."

"Let me buy you both drinks. Strawberry lemonade for you, Tess, and still white wine for you, Jen? How about you, Stevie? Another beer, Joe?" He wasn't trying to buy favor among Jenny or her friends. Just being polite, he told himself.

He was pretty sure Joe was about to eagerly accept the offer of a free drink, even though the one he had was only half-empty and even if it was being offered by a cop. But Stevie spoke up quickly. "I'm good, thanks. And, Joe, it looks like the rest of the band is getting ready to play again. You should probably join them."

"Oh. Yeah, okay. Catch you later, Gavin."

"Sure." As the other man moved away, Gavin turned toward the line at the bar. "I'll get the drinks."

"You can't carry them all by yourself," Stevie pointed out. "Jenny, why don't you help him? Tess, I see a guy I know who you might enjoy meeting. He's still married, but separated, so he's sort of eligible, right? Jenny and Gavin can find us after they get the drinks."

Gavin wasn't sure who looked more reluctant to agree with Stevie's suggestions, Tess or Jenny. Jenny's hesitation around him certainly wasn't doing much for his ego. Yet, he still couldn't seem to back away.

He placed a hand lightly on her back to keep her close to him as they made their way to the bar. He ordered the drinks and tipped the bartender.

"Thank you," Jenny murmured when he handed her the wineglass.

He sipped his beer, then asked casually, "Where's the fiancé tonight?"

Jenny's brows creased with a frown that she quickly smoothed. She glanced quickly around, as if to make sure no one had overheard his question. "He's not officially my fiancé yet," she answered quietly. "I'm not ready to make any announcements. And he's not here this evening. He's been out of town for more than a week and won't be back until Wednesday."

So her suitor had been out of town when she'd headed for the cabin to consider the proposal. And she hadn't seen him since she'd returned, meaning Gavin's had been the last kiss on her lips.

For some reason, that gave him a sense of satisfaction.

Chapter Seven

"Hi, Jenny." The woman Gavin had met when he'd first arrived—Cindy? Sandy?—rushed toward them with an avidly curious look on her made-up face. She rushed into speech before Jenny could even respond to the greeting. "I'll be coming into your store this week. I'm going on a week-long Caribbean cruise with some of my sorority sisters from college next month and I need all new beach and party clothes. Since I've started my new workout program, all my clothes are just falling off me."

"You look wonderful, Sandy," Jenny assured the woman with cheery warmth. "And make sure you come in. If I'm not in the store, tell Amber I said to give you a ten percent discount. I'll leave a note in your account file."

Sandy's face lit up. "Really? Thanks, Jen! I'll definitely stop in."

"I'm sure you'll find exactly what you're looking for. We have a whole new line of cruise wear and accessories that should meet your needs."

"I can't wait to see it." The woman eyed Gavin again, open speculation in her expression as she looked from him, then back to Jenny. "So, where's Thad this evening?"

He noted that Jenny's smile didn't waver as she answered lightly. "He's in LA on a business trip. I'll be sure and tell him you said hello. But where are my manners? Sandy Powell, this is Gavin Locke. He went to college with Stevie and me."

"We met when I arrived," Gavin replied smoothly. He wasn't thrilled about the offhanded way Jenny had introduced him, but he let it stand. "Sandy welcomed me quite graciously."

He thought he heard just a hint of a wry note in Jenny's voice when she responded, "I'm sure she did. Don't forget to ask Amber for that discount, Sandy. And let her or me know if there's something else we can do to help you prepare for your cruise."

"I'll do that. Thanks, Jenny." Perhaps Sandy decided that the discount was more valuable than digging for more gossip fodder. With a little wave, she hurried off as quickly as her tight skirt and ridiculously high heels would allow, to join a small group of women gathered nearby.

Gavin suspected there would still be some speculation about his presence at Jenny's side while the man she'd been seeing was out of town. Though he could only guess how Jenny felt about that, he decided it didn't really bother him all that much.

Moving out of the way of other thirsty guests, Jenny

looked up at Gavin with a somber expression. She opened her mouth as if to speak, but was interrupted when Tess descended on them to pluck her lemonade out of Gavin's hand.

"Thank you," she said, her smile strained. "I'm going to try very hard to pretend this is something stronger than lemonade."

Coming up behind her, Stevie sighed heavily. "Art's not that bad, Tess. Obviously he thinks you're hot. That's a good thing, right?"

Their auburn-haired friend sighed and took another gulp of her tart drink before replying. "He asked if I have any moral objections to sleeping with a man who's still technically married. He said he wanted to get that little detail out of the way before we went any further. Doesn't like wasting time, he said. And we'd barely shaken hands!"

Jenny gave a little gasp. "Seriously? Gross."

"Right?" Tess motioned dramatically with her glass, nearly splashing her drink over the rim.

"He's just going through that awkward stage between married and single," Stevie explained with a shrug. "It's been a while since he's dated and maybe he's a little…"

"Desperate?" Gavin supplied drily.

She chuckled. "Maybe. And sure, he needs to take it down a notch."

"Or a dozen notches," Tess muttered darkly. "No more attempted fix-ups tonight, okay, Stevie? Let's just enjoy the music."

The band had taken their time setting up again, chatting with one another and with some of the people hanging around the dais, but now the first chords of a song began. Some of the guests turned expectantly to pay attention, while others carried on with their avid conversations, the evening's entertainment being merely an excuse for professional and social networking. Jenny located a table with three recently vacated chairs, and Gavin snagged another from nearby, dragging it up to join them.

The volume of the music wasn't earsplitting, but it was loud enough to make conversation more difficult now. Gavin leaned back in his chair and sipped his beer, content to listen and to watch Jenny with her friends. Stevie managed to make herself heard as she chattered away, though occasionally she remembered to try to look as though she were paying rapt attention to her boyfriend's performance.

The band was good, he supposed, though their brand of wailing alternative rock wasn't really to his taste. Give him country any day. Strait, Jackson, Brooks, some of the newer stuff by Chesney, Shelton, Florida Georgia Line. He still listened to some classic Diamond Rio occasionally, though he tended to avoid the memories their songs invoked. Jenny had loved their music back in the day. Did she still, or had her tastes become more sophisticated to suit her new status?

A few people drifted out onto the smallish dance floor, followed by a few more once that ice was broken. A slightly chubby guy with thinning hair and a winning smile paused by the table. "Hi, Tess. I thought that was you. How's that boss of yours? Still a slave driver?"

She laughed. "Hi, Glenn. And yes, Scott will never change."

"Would you like to dance? Unless your lucky friend here doesn't want to share any of the lovely ladies at his table."

Gavin chuckled.

Watching as Tess and Glenn moved to the dance floor, Stevie exhaled gustily. "That's not going anywhere. No chemistry between them at all."

"Okay, I have to ask. Why are you so hell-bent on fixing Tess up with someone?" Gavin asked with a bewildered shake of his head. "Seriously, she's great-looking and seems nice enough. I wouldn't think she'd need you to round up dates for her."

Stevie wrinkled her nose. "You'd think. But she and Glenn weren't joking about her boss. Tess works *all* the time. Even more than Jenny, and Jen's a major workaholic. Tess has been saying she's ready to get married and start a family, but she's had trouble meeting anyone with her crazy hours. Online connections just aren't working out for her so far, so I hoped maybe she could meet someone here tonight on her rare chance to mingle. Um, you said you're single, right?"

Jenny groaned, but Gavin only laughed. "Yes, I'm single, and yes, I think Tess is great, but..."

"But no chemistry with her," Stevie finished with another sigh.

He made a concerted effort not to look at Jenny. "Not that I've noticed, no."

"Oh, well, if you change your mind, I've got her number."

Jenny set her wineglass down with a thump. "Seriously, Stevie."

Gavin thought it might be time to turn the tables on Jenny's meddling friend. "So what about you and Joe Porkpie Hat? Seriously?"

Stevie had never been easily offended, and apparently that hadn't changed. She merely spread her hands.

"Yeah, I know, he's kind of a nerd, but he's a very talented musician. And he's a lot of fun when he's not trying to be the cool bass player, you know? When it's just the two of us, or a few close friends, rather than a crowd like this."

"I'll take your word for it."

A new song started, a bit slower this time.

Gavin turned to look at Jenny, who was being very quiet. "How about it, Jen? Want to dance? For old times' sake?"

She had always loved to dance. He couldn't imagine that ever changing, no matter what else might be different about her now. Yet, she hesitated, leaving him to wonder if she'd tried and failed to find an acceptable reason to decline. Was she, too, afraid of the electricity he sensed sparking between them again?

He knew she'd been hurt by their breakup, maybe almost as much as he had, though that was hard to believe. He couldn't blame her for not wanting to reopen those old wounds, any more than he did. And yet…

He stood and offered her his hand. "Just one dance?"

She placed her hand in his. "Just one," she said.

He noticed that Stevie watched with a suspiciously smug smile as they walked toward the dance floor.

How could ten long years fall away in the space of only minutes? How could a decade of change and growth be forgotten with only the touch of a man's hand, the warmth of his body next to hers? How could formerly hazy memories of long, passionate, wondrous nights be suddenly more real to her than the people surrounding them as Gavin took her in his arms on the dance floor?

Jenny closed her eyes with a touch of despair as the foolish questions flooded her mind, making her stumble a bit as he guided her into the dance. Opening her eyes and glancing up at him, she murmured an apology.

Stop this, Jenny. Stop it before you do something incredibly stupid.

"Stevie hasn't really changed a bit, has she?" Gavin spoke with his mouth close to her ear to be heard over the music. His warm breath brushed her cheek, and she almost shivered, but managed to control herself.

"Of course she has. We've all changed in ten years."

He eyed her a bit too closely, as if trying to read her expression. "Okay."

"You've changed quite a bit, too," she couldn't help pointing out. "I'm sure some of your experiences as a police officer have left their mark on you, in addition to the scar on your shoulder."

If he had other physical scars from his service, she hadn't seen them, but then she'd been hesitant to look very closely. For various reasons.

"I'm sure you're right," he agreed equably. "It gets ugly at times."

She had no doubt that was an understatement. Oddly enough, she was torn between wanting to hear more about his work and being reluctant to know the grim details. She shook her head. "The thing is, we're all different now. We've all changed."

"I'm kind of hoping that's a positive thing."

He was gazing into her eyes again, and once again her thoughts scattered. She tried desperately to keep them in line.

Sex, she told herself flatly. That was all this was about. She'd always had a somewhat primitive response to whatever pheromones Gavin put out, and apparently that was one thing that had not changed. It wasn't as if she were unique in her response to him. Even women who looked quite happy to be with their own partners couldn't help glancing Gavin's way a time or two. There was something so very virile and masculine about him that no red-blooded woman of any age or eligibility status could help but notice.

Still, if he was getting ideas that there was still something between them, that their chance meeting at the cabin could lead to anything more, she needed to set him straight. Sure, they'd gotten along fine at the cabin, worked well as partners in cleaning up after the storm, shared a few meals. Shared an amazing kiss. But that was supposed to have been a kiss of goodbye, not the start of something new. And if she'd thought of that kiss a few times—more than few times—since, well, that, too, was only natural, right?

Perhaps a crowded dance floor wasn't the ideal place to remind him that it was too late for them to try to recapture the past. It was bad enough that people who knew she was dating Thad were eyeing her curiously now, wondering about the identity of this sexy guy she was dancing with and talking with so intently. Did any of them know Thad well enough that they'd be on the phone to him soon, oh-so-casually asking if he knew what was going on? He wasn't the jealous type, she acknowledged candidly, but she doubted he'd like being the subject of gossip.

Gavin's hand moved at the small of her back, pressing very lightly inward to bring her an inch closer to him. She could have resisted; he didn't hold her that tightly. But for just that one moment of weakness, she allowed her eyelids to go heavy, gave herself permission to simply enjoy the remainder of the dance without thought of what would come after. It was unlikely that she would ever dance with Gavin again. Might as well enjoy it while she could.

The music ended with a flourish of Joe's bass guitar. Swallowing a regretful little sigh, she stepped back. "Gavin, do you think we could find someplace to talk? In private?"

Looking steadily at her, he nodded. "I think that can be arranged."

She turned toward their table. Stevie had been joined by Sandy Powell and a couple of other women Jenny didn't recognize, as well as two guys who hung around the table, flirting, laughing. But she didn't see Tess among the group. Was she still dancing with Glenn? No, there was Tess, hurrying toward them, a phone in her hand and a very familiar look on her face.

"I'm so sorry, Jenny."

"Don't tell me. His Majesty needs you again."

Tess nodded somberly. "I'm afraid so. I have to leave. Do you want me to drop you off at your place on my way or…"

"I'll drive her home," Gavin cut in, his tone encouraging no argument.

Tess looked to Jenny for guidance.

Jenny moistened her lips. The thought of being driven home by Gavin made her entire body tighten with nerves. So many emotions still simmered between them. So many words that were probably best left unsaid after all these years. Yet, as she'd just told him, they needed to talk. Alone. She supposed this was as good a time as any.

She nodded. "That will be fine. Thank you, Gavin. Do what you have to do, Tess. But it wouldn't hurt you to tell His Majesty that you deserve a night off every once in a while."

"It's not another break-in, is it?" Gavin asked with a frown, slipping into cop mode.

"No," Tess assured him. "There's been an incident at one of the job sites. My boss is out of town, and the foreman hasn't been able to reach him. So they called me."

"You're on call during your off-hours?"

Tess chuckled drily. "I'm pretty much on call 24/7. It's the downside of having made myself indispensable."

Gavin lifted an eyebrow. "Maybe you should consider looking for another job?"

"I would, but…well, I love the one I have," Tess confessed almost sheepishly.

Jenny smiled. "Not to mention that she pretty much runs the company. Her title might be office manager, but the whole place would go under without her. As Scott is the first to admit."

Flushing a little, Tess shook her head. "That's hardly true. Scott is a brilliant man. He just needs a little organizational assistance."

She hurried away a few moments later to handle whatever crisis had occurred at ten o'clock on a Saturday night.

"How much later are you expected to stay at this thing?" Gavin asked Jenny.

Looking toward the gregarious Stevie again, Jenny made an on-the-spot decision. "I'm ready to leave whenever you are."

At least she didn't live far, so the drive wouldn't take

long. And she could have her little talk with him in the privacy of her apartment.

Stevie made no argument when they took their departure of her. In fact, she looked just a bit too pleased that Gavin had offered to drive Jenny home.

Jenny was definitely going to have to talk to Stevie tomorrow. She knew her friend wasn't Thad's biggest fan, but surely she wasn't trying to deliberately sabotage the relationship by throwing Gavin in Jenny's path. Why on earth would she think an ex-boyfriend from a spectacularly failed relationship would be a better match?

She and Gavin made their way through the crowded bar area near the exit door, then stepped out into the darkened parking lot. They could still hear the muted strains of Eleven Twenty-Five playing behind them. In front of them a steady stream of traffic traversed the road that ran past the restaurant, parallel to the river. Pebbles on asphalt crunched beneath their feet as they walked to Gavin's truck. He didn't speak, and she could think of absolutely nothing to say, either.

He opened the door for her, then held out a hand to give her a boost into the tall cab. She settled into the seat, arranged her dress around her legs and fastened her seat belt. Gavin climbed behind the wheel, slanted a smile at her that made her nerves flutter again, then started the engine. Country music blasted from the speakers before he quickly turned it off. Fortunately, it had been a new song and not one that carried any old baggage with it.

She gave him the name of her apartment complex and he nodded to indicate that he was familiar with it. He didn't seem to be interested in conversing as he drove, so she settled back into the taut silence and mentally rehearsed a breezy, casual speech about how nice it had been to see him again, how she was glad they'd had a chance to put the hard feelings behind them, how she would always remember him fondly even as she went on with the hard-won life she'd been leading before they'd reconnected.

"You'll turn right at the next light," she said, mostly to ease the mounting tension.

"I know." His tone wasn't curt exactly, but there was an edge to it that made her aware she wasn't the only one dealing with discomfort during this drive. She thought wistfully of how effortlessly he'd teased with Stevie and how comfortable he'd seemed with Tess, but there was entirely too much history between her and Gavin to allow them that easy interaction.

With a couple of cars stopped ahead of him, he braked for the red light, his fingers drumming restlessly on the steering wheel. She found herself mesmerized by the movement. The light must have changed and he eased forward. Because she was studying his strong hands instead of looking out the windshield, she didn't see what happened next, but Gavin suddenly braked and pulled into the parking lot of the gas station on the corner. The station was closed for the night, but one other car was parked in the lot. She noticed someone standing outside the other vehicle—a woman, she thought, but it was hard to tell in the shadows under the yellow security lights.

She frowned toward Gavin. "Is something wrong?"

"Sit tight. I'll be right back," he promised, and slipped quickly out of the truck.

She watched as he approached the other car, his

hands out in a nonthreatening position at his sides. Squinting, she saw that the woman was bent over, one hand on the top of her car and the other hand on her stomach. Either she was quite overweight, or…

Or pregnant, she realized suddenly. Despite Gavin's instructions, she reached for her door handle and jumped out of the truck to see if there was anything she could do to help.

The woman was probably close to her own age, though it was hard to tell in the pale lighting. She leaned heavily against her car, crying, gagging and moaning while Gavin talked soothingly to her. To make things worse, Jenny could hear wails from the backseat of the car, at least two separate little voices. "What's going on?"

Gavin had the woman by the elbows now, supporting her as he summed up succinctly, "She was stopped at the light ahead of us and had some sudden sharp pains and felt dizzy. She was able to pull in here and stop the car but now she's in severe pain and nauseated. I told her I'm an off-duty cop and I'll get her help. I've already called for an ambulance."

He'd done all that in the brief minutes it had taken her to even see that someone was in trouble, Jenny realized. Still speaking in the same calming tone, he supported the woman while she was sick again beside the car, and he was apparently unfazed by the unpleasant situation.

Another shriek came from the car.

"My babies," the woman gasped, taking a staggering step that way.

"My friend is going to check on the kids right after she grabs a blanket from behind the seat of my truck,"

Gavin assured her with a glance at Jenny. "I need you to lie down until the ambulance gets here. Your kids are safe for now. They're just frightened and upset."

Jenny whirled toward the truck, located a plaid stadium blanket folded neatly behind the seat where Gavin had said it would be and whipped it out onto a relatively clean patch of pavement. She'd spotted a first-aid kit, too, but couldn't imagine anything they'd need from that at the moment. Gavin was certainly prepared for anything, it seemed.

She helped him carefully lower the crying woman onto the blanket and then she opened the back driver's side door of the woman's car. Two children were strapped into car seats, the older a boy of maybe four, the younger no more than eighteen months, if that. Both were fighting their restraints and howling for their mother. It was late, and she was sure they were sleepy and scared. The baby—a girl—was closest to her, so she fumbled with the straps and buckles to take her out of the seat and cradle her soothingly as she hurried around to the other side of the car to comfort the little boy. The baby clung to her so tightly Jenny could hardly breathe. She patted the little back as she opened the second door to look in at the boy.

"It's okay," she assured him over the lessening wails of the baby in her arms. "My friend is a policeman and he's helping your mommy. What's your name?"

"M-Marcus," he snuffled. "Can I get out?"

She wasn't at all sure she could safely control two children in a parking lot this close to a street that, while mostly deserted at the moment, was often quite busy. The few cars that passed were driving too fast, and none bothered to stop to offer assistance. Unlike Gavin, most people didn't instinctively leap to help strangers on the side of the road this late at night.

"Why don't you stay in your seat just a little longer?" she suggested, bouncing the clinging baby, whose cries were down to a whimper now. "We'll get you out just as soon as we can."

The boy burst into shrieks of protest. "I want out. I want my mommy!"

The baby began to cry again, not as loud as before, but still sounding pitiful. She probably needed a diaper change, a bed and a familiar face, not necessarily in that order, and Jenny was helpless to comfort either of the unhappy siblings. Considering their mother was still crying loudly nearby, Jenny was close to bursting into tears of sympathy herself.

The sound of a rapidly approaching siren was the most beautiful music she had ever heard. Moments later, the ambulance was parked nearby and medics bustled around the woman in distress. Gavin appeared at the car door, giving Jenny an encouraging nod as he reached into the car to unbuckle the howling little boy much more easily than Jenny had freed the baby.

"Hey, buddy, I'm Gavin," he said, lifting the boy easily into his arms. "You see those guys there? They're medics and they are taking good care of your mom, okay? She's going to be fine."

Being out of the car seat was already having a positive effect on the boy's mood. He swiped at his wet, runny-nosed face with one hand as he studied Gavin's face somberly. "My name's Marcus, not Buddy. You're a p'liceman?"

"Yes, I am." Tugging a handkerchief from his pocket,

Gavin dealt with snot and tears with an efficiency that reminded Jenny that he had two young nephews.

"I got a badge," Marcus informed him. "It's at home. It's a sheriff badge. Like Woody's."

"Yeah? That's cool, Sheriff Marcus."

The boy gave a watery giggle and rested his head trustingly on Gavin's shoulder, sucking a finger and looking toward the activity by the ambulance. Alternately rocking and bouncing the baby, who'd quieted again and was starting to doze against her shoulder, Jenny looked at the strong, steady man and the frightened little boy and felt her heart turn a hard somersault. The sensation felt a lot like panic. Delayed reaction to the tense situation—or was it something else that was suddenly making her hands tremble against the little body she held?

Finally the mother was on her way to the nearest hospital, the children were handed off to anxious relatives who'd been called to the scene and Gavin's blanket was returned to him, dirty and somewhat worse for wear. He stuffed it into his toolbox to deal with later and helped Jenny into the cab again. He sighed as he started the engine, and she could tell he was tired. It had been more than half an hour since he'd jumped out of the truck.

"Just another day in the life of a police officer, even when off duty?" she asked wryly.

He gave a weary chuckle. "Yeah, I guess."

"How on earth did you realize what was going on? Before I could even see that someone was in trouble, you were already out there dealing with the situation."

Driving onto the street toward her apartment, he shrugged. "I saw her car swerving a little when she was driving ahead of us. I thought she might be a drunk driver, and I was keeping an eye out in case I needed to call it in. Then she pulled over and climbed out of her car and started puking, and I could see she was pregnant. Thought she might need some help."

She shook her head slowly in amazement. "You were so calm. I was a nervous wreck until the ambulance arrived. I thought you might have to deliver a baby right there in that parking lot."

"Wouldn't be the first time for that, either," he said with a quick grin in her direction. "But I didn't think it was that. Mike—one of the EMTs—said he thinks it's a stomach virus."

"I saw you talking with him. Another friend?"

"I've met him a time or two. He's a friend of Rob's."

It suddenly occurred to her what he'd just said. "You've really delivered a baby?"

"Just once. Back when we had that ice storm five years ago, a woman gave birth on the side of I-30 when her panicky husband hit a slick patch and got stuck in the median. I happened to be close by, so I jumped out to help. The husband and I delivered the baby, though he wasn't a whole lot of help, to be honest. They named the kid after me—well, the middle name, anyway."

"They named him Gavin?"

He laughed shortly. "They named *her* Alexandria Gavin Smallwood. They send me photos on her birthday every year. She's starting kindergarten this fall."

She smiled in delight. "That's a very sweet story."

He grunted, typically uncomfortable with her description, then turned into the drive of her apartment complex. She gave him the entry code to the gate, and her amusement faded as he keyed it in. "I doubt that all your stories about your work have such happy endings."

"No," he said, his tone grim now. "Not all of them. But I like to think everything I do in the course of my job serves the community in some way."

"I know," she almost whispered. "That was always what mattered to you most about becoming an officer. You wanted to uphold the law and serve the community. Hands-on, you said, not from the comfort of an office or a courtroom."

If it surprised him that she remembered his rationalization word for word, he didn't comment, merely nodded again as he parked in the space she indicated. "I still feel that way."

Without yet reaching for her door handle, she stared at the stairs directly in front of them that led up to her apartment. "Avery said you left the force for a while."

"That's sort of a long story," he said after a moment. "Do you want to hear it here in the truck or are you going to invite me in?"

Now she was rethinking her earlier decision. She should probably tell him what she needed to say and politely send him on his way now. When or why he'd left the force and returned was really none of her business, especially since she might never see him again, barring another surprise meeting. Inviting him up to her place, even just to talk, was certainly not the wisest course of action, considering. Some people just had that…that thing. *Chemistry*, she thought, remembering Stevie's word from earlier. It didn't mean they were meant to be together long-term, though. The same was true in reverse. Just because a connection was somewhat more serene, more understated, more cerebral, perhaps—take herself and Thad, for example—that didn't mean a couple couldn't have a long and quietly contented union. Right?

"Why don't you come in?" she said with a sigh, despite her trepidation. "We do need to talk."

Chapter Eight

Minutes later, Gavin stood inside her living room, looking around curiously. She studied her home for a moment as though through his eyes. The entire two-bedroom apartment was done in shades of cream with a select few deep-orange accents because she couldn't resist adding touches of her favorite color. Everything was arranged just so, nothing out of place, not a speck of dust on anything. Her draperies framed a beautiful view of the Little Rock skyline at night. Stevie had helped her decorate, so everything looked classic, co-ordinated, tasteful and more expensive than it actually was. Exactly the tone she'd wanted to convey. Because she knew Gavin so well—or had at one time—she suspected it looked a little too calculated for his taste.

Her grandmother loved the place. She'd brought several friends over to see it, just to preen a bit about her granddaughter's success. Thad approved, too, telling her she had excellent taste. He said he wanted to build a big home, and he wanted her to help him design it, decorate it, fill it with elegant dinner parties and intimate gatherings of vibrant conversationalists. Perhaps a couple of kids, maybe even a dog. As long as it wasn't the slobbery, shedding sort of dog, he'd added ruefully. He just wasn't the big, slobbery dog kind of guy.

Gavin loved big, slobbery dogs. His family had always had one or two when she'd known them.

"Nice place," Gavin said, the compliment obviously no more than a social formality.

"Thanks."

"I like the painting."

It hung over the fireplace, an explosion of orange from peach to near-red, a depiction of a sunset over a tropical beach. The colors refracted in the gathering clouds, bled into the waves, stained the sand, spilled over a single shell lying in the foreground. It was the only item in the harmonized decor Thad didn't care for. He thought the artist, a student Jenny had met at a local university gallery showing, had been too heavy-handed with the color. Jenny didn't agree. She'd visited Hawaii once for a conference about six years ago, and she'd seen a sunset exactly like this, so bold and bright and fiery that it had completely engulfed her, had taken her breath away. In that moment, she had been purely, deeply happy in a way she hadn't been since she and Gavin had…

She bit her lip, cutting off the thought.

Gavin turned away from the painting. "You asked why I quit the force for a while."

Despite all her internal lectures, she still found herself asking him to sit down, and she knew it was because she wanted to hear this. When it came to Gavin, she really was pathetic.

He looked so out of place on her delicate cream brocade wing-backed chair. Too big, too masculine, too colorful somehow for the neutral room. His words made that contrast even more jarring. "About four years ago, I got in the middle of a knife fight when I responded to a 2:00 a.m. disturbance at a sleazy club we're called to at least once most nights. One guy, young, barely out of his teens, had been stabbed in the chest and I knew from looking at him he wasn't going to make it. Others were bleeding. Someone pulled a gun and the shooting started just as we got there. I watched another kid go down. Saw one of my friends in uniform wounded so badly he spent two weeks in ICU. I watched the hysterical girlfriend of one of the punks pick up a knife and run at my friend who was down. I had to fire my weapon to stop her from shoving the knife into him."

He'd given the details in a flat, emotionless monotone that sounded memorized, as if he'd told the tale many times before. Only his eyes told the real story, and that one twisted her heart. "Did you...did you kill her?"

"No. But I was prepared to in order to save Bob's life."

Enormous relief flooded through her, strictly for Gavin's sake. She was glad he hadn't had to live with that. She swallowed hard. "Were you injured?"

"Nothing serious."

"It sounds like a chaotic scene, to say the least."

Still in that oddly detached tone, he agreed. "It was. Not the first I'd dealt with. Hasn't been the last."

"So what was different about that one?" she asked perceptively.

He spread his hands, his face bleak now. "I saw the eyes of the kid who'd been stabbed before we got there. He was so young. Scared, but resigned. As if that was exactly the way he'd expected to end up. And I found myself asking what was the damned point of it all? Sometimes it feels like we do the same thing every night and then come back and do it all again the next. We arrest the same people over and over, then watch them get out and go right back to what they were doing before. I started having nightmares about being unable to stop the girl from slashing Bob while he was lying there hurt and unable to defend himself. Mom was nagging me to find a safer job, Dad was sick, the father of the woman I was dating kept offering me more and more money to work for him handling security for his company in Hot Springs. So, I gave it a shot."

It didn't escape her that he'd let himself be influenced to quit by another woman, though he'd refused with her. Had it been because he'd been ready to try something different for himself that time? She pushed that question away, as it shouldn't matter to her at this point. Still, she couldn't resist asking, "The woman who shops at my store?"

He grimaced. "No, someone else."

So there had been several women after her. She supposed she shouldn't be surprised. Though she didn't think of him as a player, Gavin Locke was never going to be a monk.

"You didn't like security work?" she asked to distract herself.

"Hated it. Especially after Molly and I broke up and

it got too awkward to work for her dad. So I left that job and took one selling construction equipment for my uncle. When that didn't work out, I tried my hand at driving a delivery truck. Bored out of my mind. I thought about going back to school, maybe training to be an EMT, maybe some sort of medical technician. But when it came time to make a decision, I knew what the answer had to be. I'm a cop. I'm pretty sure I was born a cop. It's all I've ever wanted to be, all I know how to be. It's not always a nice job—it can be ugly and traumatic and sometimes even boring. It gets too little respect and damned little gratitude most of the time. But sometimes, someone names their kid after you. So, I told everyone who wanted me to do something else that I was sorry if it disappointed them, but this is what I had to do. And I'm never again going to try to change who I am just to keep someone else happy."

Gavin knew who he was. What he wanted. Where he belonged. As much as it pained her to admit it, she both admired and rather envied his certainty.

If she'd had even the most tentative thought that perhaps he'd be ready now to move on to something less hazardous, that his latest on-the-job injury would discourage him from staying on the force, she surrendered it then. Studying him through her lashes, she realized he might as well be wearing a uniform rather than his polo shirt and khakis. Even off-duty, he was all cop. And anyone who loved him would have to be willing to love that part of him, as well.

"So, anyway, there's my story for the past ten years," he said, spreading his hands. "You asked, and I've answered. I trained for my career, got a degree, had a few relationships that didn't work out, tried a couple other jobs I didn't care for and made a lot of good friends. All in all, I'm content with my life. I'm looking forward to being on the job again soon. When I take time off, I want it to be for vacation, not sick leave."

"So this latest, um, incident didn't shake your confidence." Making it a statement rather than a question, she nodded toward his shoulder.

"No. Maybe a few bad dreams the first night or two, but no more than to be expected, and I was prepared for it. I can handle my work and everything that comes with it. Just had to make sure before that I'd made the right choice."

As candid as he was being with her, Gavin wouldn't like being seen as vulnerable. Nor did she think of him in that way.

"It sounds like a good life," she said quietly, trying to smile. "Exactly what you always wanted."

"Maybe not exactly," he said, his eyes locked with hers. "But close."

She didn't know how to respond, other than, "I'm glad you're happy."

"And you? Are you happy, Jen?"

Shifting her weight on the sofa where she'd perched, she twisted the ring on her right hand, a nice costume piece from her shop. "I told you about my career when we were at the cabin. I love owning my own store, and I'm excited about the second store I'll be opening in Jonesboro. The work keeps me insanely busy, but I've enjoyed almost every minute of it."

"It was what *you* always wanted to do. Be a successful business owner, I mean."

"Yes, and I've accomplished that."

His eyebrows rose, and she wondered what he'd heard in her voice. "Why did that sound like past tense?"

She felt a muscle twitch in her jaw, a quickly suppressed grimace. "Not past tense," she assured him. "I'm just keeping my options open. I mean, I want to stay busy and productive and useful, whatever direction I take next. Even if I'm not personally overseeing the boutiques on a daily basis, I could start a charitable foundation or get involved in a political cause. Something important that would let me utilize my talents and training."

He eyed her with a hint of skepticism. "Since when do you care about politics?"

"I've always been involved in community activities," she reminded him a little too heatedly. "Even in college, I was a member and officer of several civic organizations."

"True. But mostly because you were already starting to make future business connections," he murmured, and she couldn't argue with him because he wasn't entirely wrong.

"I've matured," she said instead, both her tone and her posture a little stiff. "We all do eventually. It's important to me to try to make a positive difference, just as you do in your daily work."

"Are you thinking about selling your shops after you open the one in Jonesboro?" he asked bluntly.

Even hearing the possibility put into words made her throat tighten, but she answered candidly. "Maybe."

"Why? The boyfriend doesn't like sharing you with your work?"

And here was finally the subject they'd been avoiding, and yet was the primary reason they'd needed to talk. Gavin's tone was cutting enough to make her chin rise defensively.

"Thad would never tell me what to do with my career. But if I accept his proposal, I'd be traveling with him quite a bit and busy with a lot of things outside my boutique business. I'm not sure I'd have time to do justice to both endeavors, and you know how I feel about doing anything halfway."

"Thad Simonson, right? One of *those* Simonsons. Of Simonson, McKenzie and Ogilvie."

She nodded to confirm the long-established law firm that had jump-started so many political careers, from local offices to Washington, DC. The Simonson name was on a few buildings in the area, including a law school library, so it was no surprise Gavin was familiar with the family, though she didn't think she'd mentioned Thad's last name to him yet. She didn't ask how he knew. She and Thad had appeared together at several prominent local events during the past few months, so maybe a mutual acquaintance had mentioned to him that she'd been seeing Thad Simonson.

"Congratulations, Jen." His voice was indifferent now, deceptively so, judging by the way his eyes had darkened to a glittering navy. "You snagged yourself a lawyer, after all."

She swallowed a gasp that would have only rewarded his deliberate dig. When she was certain her voice would be steady, she said icily, "That doesn't deserve a response."

His nod might have been meant as an apology, but didn't come across as very penitent. "When's the wedding?"

Still stinging from his barbed comment, she glared

at him. "There's no date yet. As I said, I'm taking my time to make certain of my answer."

"How long have you been seeing him?"

"About seven months."

After a moment, he asked brusquely, "Are you in love with him?"

She moistened her lips. "Thad is a great guy. He and I have a lot in common, and we enjoy each other's company. I wouldn't even consider marrying him if I didn't have feelings for him."

It was a pathetically lame response and she was all too aware of it. Gavin's expression made it clear that he thought so, too. "That's not what I asked you."

Her chest tightened. Rather than continuing that line of questioning, she shut it down. "You wanted to know what was going on in my life. Now I've told you. I'm in a relationship with Thad. I don't think you need all the details."

"So were you thinking of him when we kissed at the cabin? Or when we danced tonight?"

The wave of sensations those reminders invoked stole the breath from her lungs and made her fingers clench despite her efforts. She cleared her throat before saying tightly, "For old times' sake, you said. That's all it was."

With a shrug, he pushed himself off the chair. "Yeah. Okay. Fine. That's all it was."

She stood, too, relieved that her shaky knees supported her. She didn't know why this conversation was quite so upsetting. It wasn't as if anything had really changed in her life because she'd run into Gavin a couple of times.

He moved toward the door, his steps long, purposeful. She hurried after him, though she wasn't certain what she wanted to say. "Gavin…"

Pausing at the unopened door, he turned to look down at her. "Goodbye, Jenny. I hope you have the life you and your grandmother have always wanted for you. That's exactly what you deserve."

She could tell he didn't mean the words as a compliment. She was sorry they were parting again with bitterness, but maybe that was just the way it was supposed to be between them. "Stay safe, Gavin," she whispered, reaching for the door to let him out.

He'd reached out at the same time. Their hands fell on the knob together, his atop hers. His warmth engulfed her. Both of them went very still. She wasn't sure which of them recovered first, but they both let go at once. Her hand tingled as if she'd just touched a live current. Did his?

"I'll get it," Gavin said, and opened the door for himself. "Bye, Jen."

She didn't have time to respond before he was outside, the door closing hard behind him.

Out of habit, she turned the dead bolt. And then she rested her head against the cool wood. Tears leaked from the corners of her eyes, traced slowly down her cheeks. She thought she'd shed the last of her tears for Gavin a long time ago. She should have known there would always be a few left when it came to him. She didn't even know why she was crying now.

Her feet felt heavy when she turned to take a couple steps away from the door. For some reason, she found herself looking toward the sunset painting, seeking… something from the warmth and colors. She wasn't sure what exactly. Not finding it there, she turned her head and her gaze fell onto a small, hammered silver box Thad had given her for Valentine's Day. It sat on her clear glass-topped coffee table, seeming to float above the white rug that lay beneath the table on the wood floor. In stark contrast to the riotous painting, the box was pretty, delicate, a little on the formal side.

She pushed a hand wearily through her hair, her mind spinning with doubts again.

Someone rapped sharply on the door, making her start and whirl toward it. Was there something more Gavin wanted to say? Hadn't he hurt her enough?

She opened the door slowly, her fingers trembling. She looked up at him with still-damp eyes she couldn't hide. "Did you forget something?"

Surging through the opening, he reached out to snag the back of her neck with one strong hand. "Yeah," he muttered. "This."

She heard the door close even as his mouth claimed hers in a hard, hungry kiss.

Every nerve ending in Jenny's body responded to the passion in Gavin's kiss. Momentarily paralyzed, she couldn't breathe, couldn't speak, couldn't move to either push him away or draw him closer. Her hands lay on his chest, her fingers curled into his shirt. She didn't remember resting them there. His were at her hips, holding her in place while his lips and tongue made sure she could think of nothing but him.

He broke the kiss very slowly, tugging lightly at her lower lip as he reluctantly released it. He lifted his head, his gaze burning into hers. She knew what he saw when he looked at her. Her hair was mussed, her cheeks still tear-streaked, her mouth damp and reddened. Her heavy-lidded eyes probably told him exactly how much turmoil he'd stirred in her.

"Gavin." His name came out on a whisper, and she wasn't sure if it was meant as reproach or plea.

His voice was a growl, rough but still somehow gentle. "You know all you have to do is push me away and I'm gone."

She did know that. One word, one small shove, and he would leave. And this time he wouldn't come back.

Her fingers tightened on his shirt. "I can't think when you kiss me. You confuse me."

His hands cupped her face. "You aren't confused, Jenny. You know what you want. What you've always wanted. And it isn't this," he added with a quick, dismissive glance around the room. "This sterile, impersonal, colorless place. I saw more of your personality when I went into your store the other day than I do in your home. And you're thinking of giving that up, selling the business you've planned and worked toward and sacrificed for, just to stand at some politician's side and smile?"

She started to draw back, vaguely offended that he'd disparaged the apartment she'd so painstakingly put together. Not to mention her potential lifestyle choice. "That's not what I'd be doing. Not—not most of the time, anyway."

"And this guy you can't say you're in love with? Does he like this place?"

"Yes, he does."

"Is he aware that the only real glimpse of you in this room is hanging over the fireplace?"

She bit her lip.

He eased her lower lip from between her teeth with his thumb. "Does he confuse you when he kisses you?"

"Don't," she whispered, aching for something she couldn't define.

He understood her quandary better than she did, it seemed. "Don't kiss you? Or don't tell you that I want to kiss you again? That I want to do a hell of a lot more than kiss you? That I've wanted you again ever since you fell into my bed at the cabin? That I realized I couldn't walk away without telling you?"

He rubbed the pad of his thumb slowly across her trembling mouth. "You made a point to tell me you aren't actually engaged yet. That he asked you days ago and you still haven't decided on an answer. Doesn't that tell you something? Even if I weren't here confusing you, should it really take that long to make up your mind if you knew it was the right choice for you?"

She sighed heavily, old wounds throbbing deep inside her. "Gavin, you and I—we tried it before. It didn't work. It was always too intense between us. I'm…I'm comfortable with Thad," she added, trying to make that sound more satisfying than it suddenly felt.

He shook his head and she thought she saw sympathy and understanding in his eyes now. "I didn't come back to ask you to choose between him and me. I just couldn't leave without asking if you're sure he's any more right for you than I was. The real you, who escaped to a cabin in the woods to think rather than staying in this dainty apartment. The you who gets excited about opening a second store, but looks serious and logical when talking about a proposal of marriage. The you who comes alive in my arms every time we kiss."

She swallowed a low moan.

Lowering his head a bit more, he looked deeply into her eyes. "Don't throw away everything you've worked for just because it seems like something you *should* do, Jenny. Something you'd be doing mostly to impress your grandmother and to give you a shortcut into that lifestyle you were always told you should want for yourself. Despite what I said in anger before I walked out, you deserve a hell of a lot more than that."

"I'm quite capable of making my own decisions about what's best for me," she assured him, though her heart had flinched with his words.

"You're one of the most capable and intelligent women I've ever known," he answered evenly. "But you were indoctrinated from an early age to equate money and social standing with happiness. We both know who's to blame for that."

"My grandmother has always wanted the best for me. She didn't want to see me end up like my mother, struggling and grieving," she reminded him, on the defensive again.

"I always thought she should let you make up your own mind about what's best for you."

She pulled away from him, freeing herself from his tempting touch. "I've always looked out for myself. Why else do you think I made myself walk away from you ten years ago when doing so was so hard I thought I'd never stop hurting inside? I knew I couldn't change you, couldn't persuade you to choose a safer career, but I knew also that I couldn't handle the fear and uncertainty that came with it. I walked away to protect myself and because it wouldn't have been fair for me to keep asking you to give up your dreams. And I've done quite well for myself since, I might add."

Pushing a hand through his hair, he nodded. "I never doubted you would. You've accomplished almost everything you said you wanted. Are you really considering walking away from it, Jen? He can give you every material thing you desire, but can he give you the joy and fulfillment your shops bring you?"

He lifted his hand again, resting it against her cheek, and she remained frozen in place as he lowered his head to brush his lips against hers, very lightly. No pressure, no insistence, but so much tenderness that she could feel a fresh wave of tears pushing at the backs of her eyes.

"I can feel you starting to tremble again," he murmured against her mouth. "I can almost hear your heart racing. It's always been that way between us, from the first time we touched. We're older, more experienced now, but the electricity between us hasn't changed, not for me at least. You're still the only woman in the world who can make my head spin just with a brush of your skin against mine."

A moan escaped her before she could stop it. Her knees turned to gelatin, and her pulse roared in her ears. No, she thought in despair. No one else had ever made her feel the way Gavin had. The way he still did. Kissing Thad was pleasant. Even occasionally arousing. But not like this. Never like this.

She melted into him.

This time her mouth was as ravenous as his, as bold in acting on that craving. Her fingers still gripped his shirt, but in demand now, tugging him closer, holding him there even though he displayed no interest in moving away. She nipped his lip as if in punishment for making her acknowledge this desire, and she reveled in his throaty moan that was more pleasure than protest. Her tongue dueled with his, equally angry, equally hungry, equally fierce.

Equal.

His hands left her hips to sweep over her, as if to explore the changes time had brought to the body he'd once known as well as his own. She was a bit curvier than she'd been as a teenager, but judging by his murmurs of appreciation and by the impressive hardening against her upper thigh, Gavin was more than satisfied.

She'd admired his broad shoulders and solid chest when she'd changed his bandage at the cabin, but she hadn't allowed herself to explore them thoroughly then. She did so now, sliding her hands beneath his shirt, spreading her palms against the hot skin and well-defined musculature. The bandage was gone now, as were the stitches. A thin smattering of chest hair tickled her fingers. His stomach muscles contracted sharply when she slowly followed that thinning line of hair downward toward the waistband of his pants.

He caught her hand. His voice was hoarse when he warned, "You're playing with fire, Jen."

"I've been cold for too long," she whispered, her own tone stark.

"Jenny." He pulled her into his arms, wrapping himself around her. She pressed even closer, soaking in his heat, her mouth joining his in a kiss that was less frantic now, more savoring, more tender. Her tongue stroked his rather than battling it. Her hands caressed him over his shirt, over the muscles that felt familiar yet new at the same time. She pushed away his shirt to provide her better access.

Focused solely on him, she hardly remembered moving from the living room to the bedroom. But she was keenly aware of every other detail. His hands beneath her dress. Hers tugging his shirt over his head and tossing it aside. His mouth on her throat, her shoulder, her breasts. Her fingers tugging at his belt, his zipper, eager to remove the garments between them.

Somehow he remembered little caresses that made her gasp and squirm in pleasure against the snowy bedclothes. And he'd learned some new tricks that caused her to arch and cry out helplessly as her toes curled into the tangled sheets. He took his time, teasing her and pushing her right to the edge before drawing back, slowing down. She heard an almost feral growl escape her. Even as she shoved him onto his back to retaliate, she was a little startled that the sound had come from her throat.

She used her teeth, nipped at his ear, his chin, his throat, his chest. Her hand slipped down between them, grasping him, stroking him until he was the one arching and groaning and the husky laugh of satisfaction was hers. She laughed again when he deftly flipped their positions. She landed among the pillows with her hair tangled wildly around her damp face. One pillow fell over her, threatening to smother her.

Gavin shoved the pillows off the bed and to the floor with one idle sweep of his hand, his gaze focused intently on her face. "Now?"

"Yes, *please.*"

He chuckled and kissed her thoroughly. A condom appeared from somewhere, and he donned it swiftly, impatiently, while she held her breath in anticipation. When he returned to her, she welcomed him with open arms, lifted knees and eager lips. He gathered her to him and joined their bodies with one smooth, hard thrust, then stilled for a moment to allow them both time to process the moment.

Yes. This. I remember this. This...completeness.

Shushing the little voice in her head, she wrapped herself around Gavin and allowed herself to exist solely in the moment. No past to haunt her. No future to worry her. Only this man and this bed.

He began to move, slowly, steadily. Then, at her urging, faster, more forcefully. She realized that their hands were linked at either side of her head, fingers intertwined. They'd always held hands as they approached climax. How could it still be so familiar, so natural? Her heart pounded so hard it almost hurt; her breathing was raw and ragged. Her eyelids were heavy and she wanted to close them, but she needed more to keep them open, to look at Gavin's tautly drawn face above hers. Meeting her eyes, he flashed a smile at her—and she came with a cry that was echoed mere moments later by his groan of release.

Only then did she close her eyes.

Chapter Nine

Exhausted, she slept. She wasn't sure how much time had passed when she woke with a start, but she knew she'd been dreaming. She bit her lip as bits and pieces of the dream replayed in her conscious mind. She'd dreamed of her father. Of presents he'd bought her, giggles he'd tickled from her, hugs he'd shared with her. She'd seen her mother pacing, worrying. And she'd dreamed of the day her father hadn't come home.

She was annoyed with her own subconscious. *Seriously?* Daddy dreams, now of all times? She would have liked to think even her sleeping mind wasn't that clichéd.

Opening her eyes and turning her head on the pillow, she looked somberly at Gavin. He lay on his left side facing her, a corner of the sheet covering his hips. The rest of the sheet dangled over the side of the bed to puddle on the floor. Her bed was pretty much wrecked from their activities. She'd have to strip it down to the mattress to return it to its usual immaculate state. Not that the disarray seemed to bother Gavin. His eyes were closed, his breathing even. She wasn't sure he was deeply asleep, but he was dozing.

The only light in the room came from the little lamp still burning on her nightstand. The illumination flooded softly over him, casting intriguing shadows across his tanned skin. Because he'd thrown the pillows on the floor earlier, he cradled his head on his bent arm. His hair tumbled appealingly around his face, the lamplight bringing out the gold streaks.

Her leisurely inspection paused at his right shoulder. She swallowed. Even with the stitches gone, the scar was still red and puckered. She looked away.

Reaching hastily for the white duvet crumpled on the floor by her side of the bed, she wrapped it around her body as she rose a little shakily to her feet. She caught a glimpse of herself in the dresser mirror and nearly stumbled. Who was that woman with the tangled hair, swollen mouth and wild eyes, her nude body wrapped in a coverlet? She was hardly recognizable even to herself.

She slipped into the bathroom and took her time washing up, brushing her hair and teeth, trying to put her thoughts in order along with her appearance. She donned a white robe she kept on a hook on the door and tied the sash tightly at her waist, making sure the front of the garment was securely closed. Only then did she feel somewhat prepared to face Gavin again.

He was awake when she walked back into the bedroom with her shoulders squared and her chin lifted in a show of confidence. He sat up against the headboard, his tanned skin an attractive contrast to all the white surrounding him, the sheet draped across his lap and thighs. His eyelids were still half-closed, but she knew he studied her with full alertness behind that lazily satisfied expression. "Everything okay?"

She tightened her belt again. "You should go, Gavin. It's late."

"Throwing me out?"

"I just need to be alone for a while."

He thought about that for a moment, then nodded. Unselfconscious, he rolled out of the bed and gathered his clothes. She stood for a moment staring at her tousled bed, then turned abruptly and went into the other room. Rounding the granite bar, she reached into a white-painted cabinet for a water glass. She filled it and had thirstily emptied it by the time Gavin found her.

"Would you like a glass of water before you leave?" she asked without quite meeting his eyes.

"No, I'm good. I'd kind of hoped to stay a little longer, but I can see you need time to deal with this." Spotting a pad and pen on the bar, he scribbled something on the top sheet. "Here are my numbers. Call me when you're ready to talk."

At the moment, she hadn't the foggiest idea what she would say. She merely nodded.

He hesitated, as if there were many things he wanted to discuss. But obviously he could see that she simply wasn't up to that conversation yet. He took a step toward her and rested his hands on her shoulders as he bent his head to kiss her. He didn't immediately move away when he released her mouth, but looked at her with a serious expression.

"I want to see you again, Jenny. I think that goes

without saying. But even if you decide you don't want to take another chance on us, don't let anyone else try to change you to suit them. Trust me, I've been there. It doesn't work. It only makes you miserable."

"You should go now, Gavin," she whispered. Her eyes felt suddenly hot and she did not want to cry in front of him. She needed desperately to cling to what little self-control she had left. "We will talk. But not tonight."

"Take all the time you need," he said gruffly, taking a step backward. "I'll be waiting to hear from you."

She merely nodded. With a last brush of his hand against her face, Gavin left. Only then did she allow herself to sink into a chair and bury her face in her hands.

Everything had changed tonight. All her carefully laid plans had shattered beneath Gavin's kisses. No matter what happened with him, she knew she couldn't accept Thad's proposal now.

She couldn't tell Thad over the phone, of course. He deserved a face-to-face answer to his offer. He would be disappointed, though in all honesty she doubted he would be heartbroken. Nor would he be angry; in all the months they'd dated, they'd exchanged no more than a few cross words. In all likelihood, he would wish her the best, maybe try one more time to convince her how good they'd have been together, and then he would graciously accept her answer.

Thad had a plan that would remain intact despite her decision. It wouldn't take him long to implement it with someone equally suitable as his partner. Another attorney, perhaps, or a professor or marketing executive. He had no interest in vacuous young arm candy. He claimed to be attracted to intelligence, competence and poise. She'd been pleased that he'd set his standards so high and that he thought all those flattering adjectives applied to her.

As for herself—maybe she'd known all along it would turn out this way. Not that she would find Gavin again, of course, and certainly not that the powerful attraction that had always existed between them would draw him to her bed. But maybe when she'd taken off for the woods to consider and deliberate, she'd secretly known she would be unable to commit to Thad in the way he wanted.

As Gavin had pointed out, her joy lay in the business she'd built for herself, the plans and goals she still had for it. Maybe that should be enough for her. Maybe, like her mother and grandmother before her, she was destined to be single and self-sufficient. Maybe, unlike them, she'd been fortunate enough to come to that realization without the agony of losing someone she loved and with whom she'd planned to live out her lifetime. The dread was still there, still sharp and discouraging.

She had to admit now that she didn't love Thad enough to be happy with him. But she still feared she loved Gavin entirely too much.

She had almost forgotten she'd made plans to have breakfast with Tess late Sunday morning at a new café they'd both wanted to try out. Tess sent her a text asking if they were still on, and after a brief deliberation, Jenny agreed, hurrying to get ready in time.

After a near-sleepless night in her now memory-filled bed, she wanted to get out of the apartment for a while. Tess's serene, soothing presence could be just what she required to calm her jangled nerves. She definitely needed calming before she joined her mother and grandmother for their regular Sunday dinner later that evening.

"Well?" she asked as they sat at a little table in the cute but crowded café. The tables were arranged so close together that she was almost elbow to elbow with one of the three prim-looking elderly ladies at the nearest one. From their conversation, conducted in a volume meant to compensate for the noisy room and their own poor hearing, she determined that they were indulging in a nice brunch after early church services. She wasn't interested in eavesdropping, however, choosing instead to focus on her breakfast companion. "Did you handle the big work emergency last night?"

Tess looked up from her spinach, tomato and feta quiche with a rueful grimace. "Eventually. It took me a while to reach Scott. He'd let the battery run down on his phone and I had to make half a dozen calls to finally track him down at a client dinner. He took care of everything after that."

Tess probably would have been called on even if Scott were easily reachable, Jenny thought with a slight shake of her head.

During the year and a half she'd known Tess, she'd figured out a few things about her friend's relationship with her boss. Scott Prince was a brilliant businessman who'd built his commercial construction business into a successful and rapidly growing enterprise, but the day-to-day details were left to others, usually Tess. Twenty-nine years old, she had worked for Scott for six years. He'd been just striking out on his own when he'd hired her. She'd worked her way up till from clerical assistant to office manager. No one got to Scott except through her, and everyone who worked for him was more invested in keeping her happy than him.

Tess was fiercely loyal to her employer, but the first to call him out when he got "too full of himself," as she phrased it. If she had ever had romantic feelings toward her unmarried boss, she'd never said.

At the moment, Tess apparently wasn't thinking about her own hectic life. "So," she said, deftly turning the conversation around. "Gavin drove you home last night?"

Jenny took a quick sip of her coffee to delay answering, nearly burning her mouth because of her inattention. She set her cup down carefully. "Yes."

"He seems nice."

"He is."

"I think Stevie was trying to fix me up with him, but I could tell pretty quickly that it wouldn't work even if I were interested in pursuing him."

Jenny dug a mushroom out of her omelet with her fork. "I don't really see you with Gavin."

"Considering he's still head over heels in love with you, neither do I."

Jenny's fork clattered loudly against her plate, drawing a disapproving glance from the nearby church ladies. Ignoring them, she frowned across the table at Tess. "He's not still in love with me. Until last week, we hadn't even seen each other for ten years."

"Maybe he wasn't pining for you those whole ten years, but I think seeing you again brought his feelings for you back to the forefront," Tess mused aloud. "The way he looked at you last night…well, the hair on my arms stood on end. Talk about chemistry."

Jenny swallowed a groan in automatic reaction to her

friend's words, which so eerily echoed the way she'd always privately described her own reactions to Gavin. "I'll admit there is still an…attraction between us."

"Mmm." Tess sighed a bit wistfully. "I wouldn't mind knowing what it's like to be on the receiving end of that sort of attraction."

After swallowing another, more cautious sip of coffee, Jenny couldn't resist asking, "You never had that feeling when you saw me with Thad?"

Tess grimaced. "I, um…"

"I'm asking honestly, Tess. You won't hurt my feelings, whatever you say."

After a moment, her friend shrugged in resignation. "No. I never felt that way about you and Thad. I mean, he's a very nice man. I admire him quite a bit, and I'll probably vote for him for whatever office he eventually pursues. He seems very, um, fond of you."

"But the hairs on your arm have never stood on end around us?"

"Well, no."

Jenny nodded with a touch of regret.

Tess spoke quickly. "Look, that doesn't mean you and Thad won't be very happy. I mean, marriage should be based on more than physical attraction. You and Thad have so much in common intellectually and philosophically. You make great partners. Everyone says so."

"Everyone but you and Stevie."

Tess cleared her throat. "Stevie's an incurable romantic, and I'm maybe a little too choosy for my own good. We're probably not the best judges of anyone else's relationships."

Jenny pushed away her half-eaten egg-white omelet.

"I'm breaking it off with Thad. I'm just waiting until he gets home so I won't have to do it over the phone."

Her amber eyes going wide, Tess asked, "Because of Gavin?"

"Not in the way you mean. I'm pretty sure I wouldn't marry Thad even if I hadn't run into Gavin again. Gavin just made me realize that I'm very happy with my life as it is, and that my feelings for Thad aren't deep enough to justify what I'd be giving up for him. I mean, Thad hasn't asked me to abandon my career, but he and I both know I couldn't give it the attention it requires and still be the full-time political partner he's looking for. He's on the road more than he's in town, and he's made it clear he would want me to travel with him. As much as I enjoy my time with him, I think in the long run I'd regret giving up my own goals."

Tess nodded without surprise, proving that she'd had the same doubts about Jenny's future with Thad. "So… Gavin? Did you and he talk when he took you home last night?"

To her dismay, Jenny felt her face redden. She looked quickly down at her coffee, hoping Tess wouldn't notice. She should have known better.

"Um, Jenny?"

"I'm not breaking up with Thad because of Gavin," she muttered crossly. "That's not what this is about."

"Okay. Unlike Stevie, I won't pry into what happened last night. But you know she's going to ask."

"And I'll tell her to butt out," Jenny snapped, her frayed nerves unraveling. "Yes, Gavin and I have electricity or chemistry or whatever the hell Stevie calls it, but that's just sex. Okay, maybe it's great sex, maybe once-in-a-lifetime, mind-blowing, teeth-rattling sex, but that's not enough to build an entire future on. Because it wouldn't—it couldn't—always be that good, right? And then what would we have?"

Tess cleared her throat.

Realizing she'd spoken with a bit more passion than she'd intended, Jenny bit her lip. The three gray-haired ladies at the next table stared at her with wide eyes and open mouths. And then one of them grinned and winked at her.

Jenny covered her face with her hands. She had never been so happy to hear Tess's phone beep than she was at that moment.

Tess read the text message on her screen, then exhaled heavily. "As much as I would love to continue this fascinating conversation, I have to run. Duty calls. But, um, maybe you should calm yourself a bit before you speak to Stevie."

Jenny groaned into her hands. Perhaps having breakfast with a friend hadn't been the best idea today, after all. Clearly it would take more time than she'd expected to recover her characteristic composure that had been shattered last night. She would go home and work on that before she spoke with Stevie.

She would most definitely have to get a grip before she saw her mother and grandmother that evening, a meal she wasn't looking forward to at all.

Though Gavin had promised himself he would wait for Jenny to phone him, he kept second-guessing that decision as Sunday crawled by. Maybe he should call her, just to make sure she was okay. But he'd told her he'd give her time.

Though he hadn't heard a ring, he checked his phone

for missed calls Sunday afternoon, vaguely disappointed to see that there were none from Jenny. Was she waiting for him to call her? Had she talked to that other guy yet today?

Had last night been a one-time thing, an impulsive trip to the past, a way for Jenny to get him out of her system for good before moving on? Before making what Gavin was certain would be the biggest mistake of her life?

Surely she would break it off with Thad now. She couldn't marry some other guy after what she'd shared with him last night, could she? No one else could possibly make her feel what he did, just as the reverse was true for him. She couldn't even considering marrying someone else when all it took was a touch, a kiss, to ignite a blazing fire between them. Could she?

"Hey, Gav, break's almost over." Holding a basketball and wearing shorts and a tee, Avery approached. "You are still playing, right?"

Gavin stashed the phone in his gym bag again. He, Avery and J.T. had been playing Rob and a couple other medics in three-on-three basketball. The score was tied at two wins, and they'd agreed to play a twenty-one-point tiebreaker. "I'm coming."

"You weren't thinking of calling her, were you?" Avery asked suspiciously. He didn't bother to clarify who he'd referred to, as there was no need. Gavin hadn't told his friend about last night, but somehow Avery knew something was up.

"Let it go, Avery. Let's play basketball."

"Damn it, Gav, why are you letting her do this to you again?"

"Just give me the ball. The way you're playing this

afternoon, the medics are going to kick our butts this time."

"I'm not the one who got distracted and let the ball hit me in the jaw," Avery reminded him irritably. "One guess who you were thinking about."

Gavin scowled and rubbed his chin.

"Hey, guys, come on. Let's get this massacre over with," one of Rob's friends called out. "I've got to be home in time for dinner."

"Drop it," Gavin said when Avery started to speak again. "Just play ball."

With a gusty exhale, Avery spun on one athletic shoe and stalked toward the court with Gavin following. Gavin didn't really blame his buddy for being so pushy. Avery had been there to see what the last breakup with Jenny had done to him. Just as Gavin had been there during Avery's painful divorce from his first marriage a few years ago. He would give anything to make sure his friend wasn't hurt like that again. Avery certainly felt the same about him.

His friends wanted the best for him, he thought with a sigh. Maybe he should listen to them.

Maybe he'd call Jenny after this game.

Or maybe he'd wait and let her call him.

Damn it, Avery was right. He really was letting her mess with his head—and his heart—again. If he had a lick of sense, he'd forget he ever ran into her again. But when it came to Jenny, he'd never had a great deal of sense.

"So I told Margaret this morning after Sunday school that I don't care what her grandson's excuses are, there's no way I'd spend any more hard-earned money to bail out his sorry butt if I were her," Gran proclaimed over dinner, completing a story that had droned on endlessly through salad and now to the ham and potatoes course. "They've spoiled that boy something terrible and now the whole family's paying the price for it, especially Margaret, since she's the only one of the bunch who had enough sense to put away a little money for her latter years."

Jenny's mother shook her head in disapproval. "I feel sorry for Angie and Don. They don't deserve to be punished this way. But Angie still makes excuses for him, blaming all his problems on everyone but him. She can't accept that he's a grown man in his twenties now, and that he has to take responsibility for his own failings."

As uncomfortable as she was by the gossip, Jenny was relieved that at least they were focused on someone other than her for now.

Maybe the thought had crossed her mind too soon. Her grandmother turned to smile smugly in her direction. "I told Margaret that I hated to brag, but I was glad I haven't had to deal with that sort of disappointment from my grandchild. I said that Jenny hasn't given us a day's trouble since her little college rebellion, and even that was fairly mild and short-lived. Only natural, I suppose, for a teenager to test her wings when she's away from home, but we'd given her enough solid raising that she straightened up with only a little guidance from us."

Wincing at the indirect reference to Gavin, Jenny said peevishly, "I'm right here, Gran. Must you talk about me as if I weren't?"

"Just telling you what I said to Margaret."

"Well, you shouldn't have. She's upset about her grandson, and it seems unkind to boast about me to her. Besides, I'm hardly perfect." Nor was she a posses-sion to be pulled out and shown off, she added silently. It wasn't the first time she'd felt that her grandmother saw her that way.

For years, she'd tried to please her exacting grand-mother, who had dealt out gestures of affection like earned rewards.

Jenny's mom had been more generous with her af-fection, but as a hospital nurse, her hours had been very long, leaving Jenny more often in her grandmother's care. Her mom was also quieter, often overshadowed by her forceful parent, so it had been Gran who had most inspired trepidation in Jenny. Funny how those deeply ingrained patterns could carry over into adulthood, she mused as she played with the food she didn't want but was afraid to push away for fear of rousing her grand-mother's suspicions.

"Margaret understands that I was only expressing my gratitude that I've been blessed with a more successful grandchild," her grandmother shot back, oblivious to the offensiveness of her comment. "At least I know I won't have to worry about my bank account being drained by irresponsible family members. Both you girls have worked hard for your livings, and once you marry Thad, I'm sure you'll make sure your mother and grandmother have what we need, won't you, sweetheart?"

It was another not-so-subtle reminder of how selfish Jenny would be if she didn't take advantage of an oppor-tunity her grandmother had prepared her for all her life.

"I will always do everything I can to take care of you and Mom, Gran," Jenny replied carefully.

So far, her popular boutique had proven satisfactorily lucrative, and she hoped her new venture in the northeastern part of the state would be as successful. She had ideas for more stores in Conway and Fayetteville, two other Arkansas college towns with demographics that suited her line of youthful, trendy, high-end merchandise. She knew the risks of opening new businesses, but she had prepared herself as thoroughly as possible for this venture. She knew about budgeting, advertising, creating buzz on social media, targeted selection of merchandise. She'd reassured herself often that she would be able to put that training to good use as Thad's wife, but now she wondered how she could have even considered voluntarily giving up the business she loved.

She wanted to believe she'd have come to her senses eventually on her own. But if Gavin hadn't been at the cabin that weekend, would she actually have convinced herself that providing security for herself and her family outweighed her personal desires? Would she have allowed herself to be swept into a marriage with Thad that might have proven successful, but never truly fulfilling? A tiny part of her wondered...

"Jenny, is everything okay?" her mother asked quietly as they cleared the table after dessert. "You seem so distracted this evening."

"I'm sure she's missing Thad," Gran answered, complacently certain of her accuracy, as always. "Perfectly understandable, Jenny, but don't mope. It isn't becoming."

Jenny drew a deep breath and held it for a moment before replying, "I'm not moping. Just a little tired. I didn't get much sleep last night."

"You work too hard," her mother fretted. "Why don't you sit in here with your grandmother and I'll clean the kitchen?"

"I'll help you clean up, Mom," Jenny countered quickly. "It's the least I can do after you cooked this delicious meal."

"I want to watch television, anyway," Gran proclaimed. "You know I always watch my program at this time every Sunday night. Jenny's not interested in it, so she can help you."

Carrying with her the tiny glass of red wine that had been part of her nighttime routine for the past forty years or more, Gran retired to her bedroom with restrained cheek kisses for her daughter and granddaughter. She was the early-to-bed and early-to-rise type, so this was good-night. It was with some relief that Jenny watched her leave the room without any further discussion of Thad. Soon enough she would have to tell her grandmother that there would be no fancy society wedding, but she wasn't ready to deal with that tonight.

She and her mother talked of inconsequential things during the brief cleanup. Summer trends at the shop. A party her mom's hospital coworkers had thrown for a retiring administrator. Afterward, they moved out to the patio to sit in gliders, her mom with a cup of hot herbal tea, Jenny with a mug of coffee.

Her mom nodded toward Jenny's steaming mug and shook her head. "I don't know how you can drink that this late and still get any sleep."

"One cup after dinner doesn't usually affect me."

"I know. You got that from your father. He could drink strong coffee right up until bedtime and still sleep like a log for a good six or seven hours, the most he ever needed." She laughed softly at the memory, her expression suddenly looking far away.

Jenny bit her lip and ran a fingertip idly around the

rim of her mug. She and her mom never talked about Jenny's dad when her grandmother was around. Probably because Gran always had something disparaging to say about her late son-in-law.

"Honey, are you sure there's nothing wrong? You look so unhappy."

"I'm not unhappy, Mom. I'm just, well, a little distracted."

Her mom sighed. "It's Gavin, isn't it? Ever since you ran into him again, you seem troubled. Mother was livid that he came back into your life even for a brief encounter, but she's convinced herself since that you haven't given Gavin another thought. That you are totally committed to Thad. I haven't been so sure."

Jenny turned her head to look at her mother. Though she knew her grandmother couldn't possibly overhear, she spoke quietly when she said, "I'm not going to marry Thad, Mom. I'm sorry if you're disappointed, but I just can't go through with it."

If there was a momentary wistfulness, it was well hidden when her mom said flatly, "You have to make the decision that's right for you, Jenny. If you don't love Thad with all your heart, then you shouldn't marry him. It wouldn't be fair to either of you."

Jenny could imagine how her grandmother would snort in derision at such a sentimental remark. She would be sure to point out that Jenny was quite fond of Thad and vice versa, and that was a perfectly adequate foundation for a successful marriage.

"As for whether I'm disappointed, you mustn't even think that, dear," her mom added warmly. "Nothing you could do would ever disappoint me. You've been the best daughter I could ever have imagined, and I am so proud of you. I wouldn't change a thing about you. I know your father would be proud, too."

"I hope he would," Jenny murmured. "I wish I remembered him better. I was so young when he died."

"We both were. I was too young to be widowed and you too young to be left fatherless. Even in my grief, I was angry for a time that he was so reckless and irresponsible, that he died doing something so wild and foolish. I let Mother poison my mind against him for a few years, and I regret that now. I should have talked about him more to you despite her disapproval, kept him alive for you. Kevin was a good man and I loved him madly. I've never been able to feel that same way about any other man."

Staring somewhat fiercely into her cup, Jenny said, "That's so sad. That you've had to live all these years with the pain of losing him, I mean."

"Of course I wish he'd been with us longer, but despite whatever my mother says, I don't regret marrying your father, Jenny. I knew when I fell in love with him that he would never play it safe. He was a charming daredevil, what they now refer to as an adrenaline junkie, but he was also loving and kind and generous. Too generous sometimes. Money meant very little to him. But he had a heart as big as the sky, and he adored us. He even tolerated my mother. He said we should understand that her bitterness was rooted in pain and disappointment. He never failed to kiss her cheek when he parted from her, even when she batted him away. He even teased a smile out of her a few times. She cried when he died, though she tried her best to hide her tears from me, and then she just grew more bitter that another man she'd started to care for had left us too soon and in a financial bind."

That must have cemented her grandmother's hard-earned belief that it was better to marry for security than for love, Jenny thought sadly. No wonder Gran hadn't allowed herself to like Gavin, and that she promoted Thad.

"Have you told Thad yet?" her mother asked gently.

"No. I'm waiting until he gets back. Please don't tell Gran yet. I'll deal with her tantrums when it's all settled."

"Of course. I'm glad you felt comfortable talking to me."

"You've always been there for me when I needed you, Mom."

"And I always will be."

"If you need anything, anything at all, I'm doing fairly well with the store, you know. I have a little put away…"

Her mother stiffened. "Jennifer Gayle Baer, if you're implying that I wanted you to marry Thad for his money, or that I expect you to support me when I am perfectly capable of supporting myself, then I'm going to be very offended."

Smiling a little, Jenny held up a hand. "I wasn't implying anything of the sort, Mom." Though she was a little relieved to have it spelled out. "I just wanted you to know I'm here for you, too."

"I do know that. Thank you."

They glided and sipped in silence for a moment, and then her mom asked the inevitable question. "What about Gavin?"

"I don't know," Jenny admitted. "He... I have to admit there are feelings, but..."

More than anyone, perhaps, her mother understood. "But he's still a cop."

Jenny nodded somberly. "And I still don't know how to deal with that."

"Lots of jobs carry risk. He could be a pilot. Or a soldier. Or he could be a firefighter, like your dad. I always worried about the danger in his job, though sadly his off-duty hobbies were even more dangerous," she added with a little break in her voice. Speaking more firmly, she continued, "Actually, construction jobs are quite hazardous. Take it from someone who worked in ER for several years and saw some fairly nasty construction injuries. Would you be just as wary of Gavin if he were a roofer or a high-rise worker at the end of a harness? Or would you feel free to love him only if he worked in an office or a classroom, where he'd be relatively safe barring an unexpected illness or car accident or tornado or mugging?"

So many things to go wrong, Jenny thought with a little shudder. So many ways to lose someone. She knew her mother had been driving home a point, but rather than reassure her, the list only made her more afraid to give her heart completely.

"I'm scared," she whispered. "It didn't work out last time, and it almost broke my heart. What if...?"

She swallowed a huge lump in her throat.

"As I said before, you have to decide what's right for you, Jenny. Whether it's Gavin or Thad or life as a single career woman, whatever makes you happy is what you should choose. Not what pleases your grandmother or me or your friends or anyone else. Think about what it is that gives you pure joy—the way your father did for me—and go after it with your whole heart. I have no doubt that you can do anything you set your mind to. And don't worry about your grandmother. She'll throw a tantrum, but we'll deal with her together."

"Thanks, Mom."

"Any time, sweetie. I love you."

"I love you, too." And despite everything, Jenny loved her contrary, bossy, pretentious and damaged grandmother. Which only went to show, she supposed, that there was no logic to her heart. Now if only she could decide whether to listen more to her heart or her mind, her courage or her fears, when it came to Gavin.

Chapter Ten

Her tensely awaited reunion with Thad could only be described as a dark comedy of errors. Almost everything that could go wrong did.

Before he'd even left on his two-week trip, they had arranged for her to accompany him to an important fund-raiser Wednesday evening at an exclusive downtown hotel. The tickets had cost a thousand dollars each, but Thad hadn't blinked at the price. It was important, he'd said, for him to attend this particular event. All his law-firm partners would be there, and his presence was expected.

The plan had been for his plane to land early that afternoon, giving him time to go home, shower and change and pick up Jenny for a nice dinner before the gala. That schedule didn't leave a lot of time for the conversation she needed to have with him, but she was prepared to talk with him as soon as he arrived to collect her. She would be dressed to go out, but she would assure him that she would understand if he'd prefer she stay behind.

She rather hoped that would be his decision, which would be far less awkward, but she'd promised to accompany him and she would keep her word if he wanted her at his side for one final event. She knew Thad would smile and mingle and be a courteous escort regardless of his feelings about her turning down his proposal.

She hadn't heard from Gavin since she'd pretty much kicked him out of her bed. She knew he was waiting for her to call, but she wasn't quite ready for that. She told herself it was because she needed to settle things with Thad, but she suspected it was more cowardice than courtesy that held her back.

She still wondered if it wouldn't be better for both of them to leave it as it was. At least this time they would have parted with a few hours of amazing pleasure rather than angry words, with kisses instead of tears. Wouldn't that be infinitely preferable to trying again and probably failing again?

Thad called from the airport in Phoenix. His connecting flight had been delayed an hour. An hour later he called to say he'd been delayed again. Just before he was finally able to board, he gave her a quick, terse call to let her know there would be no time for dinner.

"I hate to do this, but I'll have to pick you up in a rush to make it to the fund-raiser at a decent time. I'm so sorry, Jenny."

So their talk would have to wait until later in the evening. "It's okay," she assured him. "You couldn't help the delays. I'll be ready to go as soon as you arrive."

"Thanks, sweetheart. I'll make it up to you, I promise. The attendants are telling us to turn off our phones now, so I have to disconnect. I'll see you in a few hours. Love ya, Jenny."

He disconnected before she could respond, though she didn't know what she'd have said. Why had she not noticed before how empty the words sounded from him?

She was ready an hour early, dressed in a tasteful black, knee-length dress with an unexpected pop of hot pink in glimpses of lining at the swirling hem. The dress came from her boutique, as she would be sure to tell anyone who complimented her.

Thad wore an apologetic smile when she opened her door to him. Despite his hectic hours of travel, he was impeccably groomed, as always.

"I'm so sorry to rush you this way, Jenny," he said, brushing a careful kiss close to her mouth so as not to smudge her lipstick. "You look beautiful, as you always do. Did you have dinner?"

She hadn't been able to eat a bite, but she merely nodded. "I'm fine, thanks. And again, the delays weren't your fault."

"We should go, then."

She buckled herself into the soft leather seat of his sports car while he rounded the hood after closing her door for her. Climbing behind the wheel, he shot her a smile as he started the powerful engine. "We'll have a good time tonight, I'm sure. We've gotten off to a harried start because of the inefficiency of modern air travel. I'm thinking about investing in a private jet, perhaps shared with a couple of partners. Some of my associates do that, and it's so much more convenient for them."

"I can see where it would be."

Private jets, she thought with a tiny shake of her head. She rarely even traveled first class.

He didn't speed as he drove them toward downtown, but he hovered right at the limit. "You have to admit it will be easier after we're married when we have only one home from which to operate. No more hasty pickups and drop-offs. Won't that be better?"

She almost bit her lip, but remembered at the last moment to guard her makeup. Instead, she looked out the window at the familiar landscape they passed. Though she sensed Thad glancing her way, probably wondering what was going on with her tonight, he seemed to understand this wasn't the time or the place to ask.

A small crowd of student-age demonstrators carrying signs and chanting circled outside the hotel entrance, blocking traffic and generally causing a disruption. Jenny saw several uniformed police officers trying to corral the group off the street, but it looked as though they were trying to herd cats. Defiant cats.

Thad pulled into the portico, where a slightly harried parking valet hurried to open the door and take the keys. Someone snapped a photo using a bright flash as Thad helped Jenny out of the car. Local press covering the event, most likely. Thad would have been instantly recognized. She could already imagine the cutline: Prominent Attorney Thad Simonson and Guest.

Shouts broke out from the street and she turned curiously, as did Thad and everyone else waiting to enter the fund-raiser. Some of the protesters had turned violent in their resistance to being restrained. Fists flew as more uniformed officers converged on the scene. One particularly large demonstrator threw a hard punch, sending an officer flying backward to land with a grunt of pain on the street only a couple feet from where Jenny stood.

Instinctively she took a step forward, thinking she recognized something about the man in the uniform, her heart skipping a beat in dread. It started again with a jolt when he climbed angrily to his feet and she realized it wasn't Gavin. Of course it wasn't. He hadn't even returned to work yet, she thought with an exasperated shake of her head.

Thad followed her gaze, then gave her a searching look. "Someone you know?"

She shook her head. "No."

An ambitious public defender Jenny had met a couple times before, and disliked considerably, glared at the melee and motioned dramatically to her companions as they waited impatiently to be admitted to the high-security event. "That'll just get the other uniforms riled up," she said with a long-suffering sigh. "They'll be breaking out the riot gear. I certainly hope they don't resort to excessive force just because a few protestors get out of hand. We've all seen how cops can behave."

Jenny spun on one heel to face the woman, incensed on behalf of the officers who were already succeeding in calming the scene, though several angry youths were being led away in restraints. "Protecting us, you mean? Getting punched in the face so that we can go into our thousand-dollar-a-plate gala without being harassed by people who are obviously unhappy about something? Helping women and children in distress, protecting property, keeping criminals off the streets?"

She realized belatedly that her disdainful comments would not be appreciated by this conservative crowd of politicos who at least gave lip service to supporting men and women in uniform.

The other woman gave a quick, strained laugh and apologized insincerely. "I guess I didn't word that very well. I certainly wasn't casting a bad light on all officers, merely expressing concern that this protest doesn't get out of hand on either side. Oh, look, the line's finally moving. We should go inside."

A little embarrassed now by her own vehemence, Jenny looked apologetically at Thad as he rested a hand on her back to accompany her inside. "I'm sorry. I didn't mean to cause a scene."

He chuckled. "Far be it from me to criticize you for taking a stand on a subject that's important to you. You've heard me get wound up over a few issues myself, right? I can't consider going into politics without being aware that I'll be called on frequently to defend my beliefs."

He was such a nice guy, she thought wistfully. A great catch, as her grandmother had insisted so often. And yet…his hand on her back didn't make her pulse race or her hands tremble. She wasn't in love with him—not in the way her mother had described loving her dad, or the way Jenny had loved Gavin all those years ago. The way she still loved him now.

Both men had strong convictions and noble causes. But only one of them held a permanent place in her heart. Now if only she could find the courage to open that wary heart to him, despite the risks of loving without reservation.

Fortunately, they weren't required to stay long at the fund-raiser. Satisfied to have made an appearance, and connections, Thad made excuses early, blaming weariness from travel and early appointments the next day. He offered to take her someplace for a late dinner after they made their escape, but Jenny politely declined. They made the drive back to her place in near silence.

No one had ever accused Thad of being oblivious. He waited only until they were inside her apartment before asking quietly, "You've made your decision, haven't you? About my proposal, I mean."

She moistened her lips. "I have."

He nodded in resignation. "You're turning me down."

"I'm sorry, but I can't marry you, Thad. I think you're a very special man, and I'm extremely flattered that you asked me, but it wouldn't be fair for me to accept when I don't truly believe it's right for either of us."

He sighed lightly. "I still think we'd have been a great couple. But I accept your decision, of course. I'm sorry it didn't work out."

"So am I," she said candidly, a hard lump in her throat.

Thad squeezed the back of his neck, then dropped his arm and straightened his shoulders. "If you don't mind my asking—who is he?"

"Who is who?" she asked cautiously, studying him through her lashes.

Smiling crookedly, he shrugged. "I was told you were with another man at a bar last weekend. I thought perhaps it was just a friend, but something I've heard in your voice when we've talked since made me wonder if there was more to it. Now I suspect I was right."

She cleared her throat before answering candidly. "I *was* with someone Saturday night. It wasn't planned exactly. I wasn't sneaking around seeing anyone behind your back or anything like that. I fully intended to tell you everything when you returned." *Well, maybe not everything.* "You remember me telling you about the guy I dated in college?"

He looked as though a lightbulb went on in his head, perhaps as he recalled her little speech before the fundraiser. "The one who became a police officer?"

She hadn't told him much more than that when they'd exchanged a few tales of past loves over dinner and drinks one night not so long ago. Maybe one too many drinks. "Yes."

"You're seeing him again?"

"We sort of ran into each other. It's a long story, and I'll spare you the details. But Gavin isn't the main reason I have to turn down your proposal, Thad. I don't know for certain if he and I will continue to see each other. It's just, well, I've realized that it wouldn't be fair of me to marry you when I'm not able to totally commit to you. I can't walk away from my business. Sink or swim in the long run, it means too much to me. And I couldn't do justice to you if I'm not free to travel and attend all these functions with you and everything else you need from a wife and a partner in your future. I'm sorry. I hope we can still be friends," she added, because such a speech was always supposed to conclude that way.

"I hope so, too." He leaned over to brush a kiss across her lips. "Be happy, Jenny. And if you change your mind...you know where to find me."

She wouldn't change her mind, she thought as she closed her door behind him. And he knew it. She doubted it would be long before he started seeing someone else. And while it made her a little sad to think that their relationship was over, she had no other regrets about her decision.

Apparently she was more like her mother than she'd ever realized. And despite what her grandmother or anyone else might think, maybe that wasn't such a bad thing, after all.

The drive up the hill to the cabin was much nicer in pretty weather. Emerald-green leaves rustled in a slight breeze against a brilliantly blue, cloudless sky on this Saturday afternoon. A few trees showed fresh gashes from having limbs broken off in the storm winds earlier in the month. The road was still bumpy, pocked with new holes left from the floodwaters. Much tamer now than it had been when she'd seen it last, the river ran cheerily alongside the rising road. The only storm raging now was the one inside Jenny's heart as she neared the cabin.

This was probably the most reckless thing she had ever done in her life. And it frightened her to her toes. But here she was.

She parked in front of the cabin. She didn't see anyone around, but she knew Gavin was here.

She climbed slowly out of the car, her new, bright green sneakers crunching against the gravel drive as she moved toward the front door. It was a warm day, and she'd dressed accordingly in a sleeveless top and cropped pants. A bag of similarly casual clothing sat in the backseat of her car. She was prepared to stay overnight, if things went well.

She was just about to knock when a hammering sound from around back caught her attention. Following the sound, she stepped off the porch and walked around the cabin. Gavin had his back to her as he hammered at something he was building with long wooden boards.

"At least I'm not waking you up this time," she said, speaking over the noise. "But you did look very appealing all rumpled and sleepy."

He froze, then turned slowly to face her, the hammer dangling at his side. He still looked sexy as all get-out in his loose jeans and damp tee, both covered in sawdust. "Jenny?"

It was taking everything she had to keep her posture relaxed, her tone casual, her smile easy. "What are you building?"

For a moment, he looked as though he couldn't remember. "A window box," he said after a pause. "My mom thought some flowers would look nice under the kitchen window."

"She's right. It would look nice."

He shook his head, impatiently putting an end to small talk. "Jenny, why are you here?"

"I don't like having important conversations over the phone," she replied with a shrug. "I tracked down Rob to ask him where I could find you and he told me you were here doing a little maintenance in preparation for your summer renters. I thought about waiting until you were back in Little Rock, but then I decided to invite myself to join you here. I can leave, if you'd rather be alone."

He dropped the hammer and dusted off his hands without looking away from her face. "I saw your picture in the paper a couple days ago. Avery made sure to show it to me."

She knew which picture he meant. The photographer had caught her smiling up at Thad as he'd helped her out of his expensive car. Stevie had told her it was the fakest smile in the entire history of fake smiles, but most people would probably not have realized that at first glance. Had Gavin?

"Wasn't that sweet of Avery?" she asked with an equally false smile now.

"Not particularly. You looked beautiful, by the way. I'm sure your boyfriend was very proud to have you there with him."

"Thad's not my boyfriend." She'd cried herself to sleep that night, not because she'd been brokenhearted over her breakup with Thad, but because she'd been so confused about what to do about her overwhelmingly intense feelings for Gavin. That wasn't something she would admit now. Probably ever. "He and I agreed to remain friends, but we aren't seeing each other anymore."

Gavin went very still. "Is that why you're here? To tell me you aren't going to marry him, after all? Took you a few days to get around to letting me know, didn't it?"

"I needed some time to think," she admitted. "I didn't want to rush into anything without making sure I knew what I was doing. I'd already hurt one person, though I expect he'll recover soon, and I infuriated my grandmother, who might take a little longer to get over it. So I wasn't going to come to you until I was sure I wasn't being too impulsive. Until I'd had a chance to overcome my fears and decide I could handle trying again with you, if you're still interested."

"I don't understand why it scares you so much. I mean, yeah, my job carries a risk, but so does…"

"So do firefighting and race-car driving and construction work and piloting," she cut in with a wry smile. "My mom reminded me lately that there are few guarantees in life. But I'm not going to lie, Gavin. I'm still scared."

"Of ...?"

"Of you. Of everything about you," she confessed. "Of loving you and losing you, either on the job or off. Of spending the rest of my life missing you and grieving for you, the way my mom has for my dad. The way Gran did when her husband died. I'm afraid of loving you so much I lose myself, the way I almost did in college. You warned me about giving up too much for Thad, but there was always a part of myself I held back from him. I could never hold anything back with you. And that's terrifying."

He shook his head as he took a step closer. "You honestly think I don't understand that? Seeing you again in my cabin scared the crap out of me, because the minute I did I knew I still wanted you. It took me so damned long to get over you the first time. You think I wanted to go through that again? I've tried to change to please other people before, to please *you* before, and it never worked. And yet I was half-afraid that if you asked me again, I actually might try one more time, just to be with you. Even knowing it would only lead to failure again."

Another step brought him even nearer. "And do you really think I don't worry about losing someone I love to an accident or an illness or any of the other tragedies that strike good people every day? Things I see every day on my job? Loving someone is accepting that risk, Jenny. It's learning how to push the fear aside and to enjoy every day together, just in case."

She swallowed a lump in her throat, but spoke as lightly as she could manage. She knew he wouldn't want her to get too maudlin. "That's very deep."

"Yeah, well, I'm a complicated guy."

Her lips twitched, though he wasn't smiling. "You are at that."

She reached out to him, needing desperately to touch him. Kiss him. "Gavin…"

He held her off, his face so stern that for a moment her heart stopped. Had he changed his mind? Had he decided she'd hurt him too badly the last time for him to ever trust her again? Had he concluded that it would be foolish to try again after so much time had passed?

His eyes held hers. "I'm not a daredevil, Jen. I don't take unnecessary risks on the job or for fun. I can't promise nothing bad will ever happen to me, but I can assure you I'll take every reasonable precaution. You have to decide right now if you can deal with that. If you can take me exactly as I am."

"I'll take you however I can get you," she answered quietly, beginning to breathe again. "That's what I came here to tell you. That I know now that we're right for each other, just as we are."

His eyes warmed as the faintest hint of a smile curved his firm lips. "We were never wrong for each other, Jen. We were just together at the wrong time. Before each of us knew who we really were and what we wanted. We know now. I'd never stop you from going after your dreams. I'll support you in whatever you choose to do, even if it's to enter politics yourself. Hell, you're as qualified as that pretty boy in the photo. If you want to open a whole chain of boutiques, I'll back you in that, too. All I ask is that you offer the same support for my career, even if it's not what you'd planned for your life."

"Sometimes plans change," she said, blinking back

a haze of mist from her eyes. "I'm trying to learn to be more flexible. And to appreciate surprises."

He surged forward, taking her in his arms and spinning her around. Clutching his shoulders, she laughed, not caring that he was grubby and a little sweaty from his work. She was definitely learning to appreciate surprises, she thought as his mouth closed over hers.

The cabin bedroom was dark, not from lack of electricity this time, but because they hadn't bothered turning on the lights as one hour blended into the next in the big bed. Sated and exhausted, they lay tangled together on even more tangled sheets, bare skin pressed to bare skin, heart beating against heart.

"Gavin?"

"Mmm?" The sound was a sleepy, satisfied murmur in the shadows.

"As much as I love this cabin, I'm still going to want to vacation somewhere with room service and a pool occasionally. Maybe even a spa that offers facials and massages."

He chuckled lazily. "I could appreciate that sometimes myself, but I wouldn't mind you taking Stevie and Tess for an occasional pampered weekend while the guys and I gather here for poker and beer. Or Scrabble and beer, if it's up to J.T.," he added drily.

She appreciated that he still saw them having interests of their own even as they built a life together. Tomorrow they would return to Little Rock, where he would reintroduce her to his mother and she would present him to her welcoming mother and her sullen grandmother. Gran would either accept Gavin eventually or she wouldn't. Jenny couldn't let her grand-mother's wishes guide her anymore.

"Jen?"

"Mmm?"

He rose on one elbow, and she could see him just clearly enough to tell that his expression was very serious now. "We're all-in this time, right? No more getting scared and running away?"

"I wouldn't have come here today if I wasn't ready to fully commit to you," she answered evenly.

"I'm in, too. And to prove it…"

He turned to rummage in the nightstand drawer, from which he drew out a small box. "I dug this out after I left your place the other night. I'm not sure why exactly, but I've been carrying it ever since. Maybe in the hope that I'd finally have the chance to give it to you. I've wanted you to have it for more than ten years now."

Sitting against the pillows with the sheet tucked beneath her arms, she blinked a little when he turned on the lamp. "What is it?"

"It belonged to my dad's mother. I inherited it when I was just a teenager. I was going to give it to you for your twenty-first birthday, but, well…"

She bit her lip. They'd broken up two weeks before that birthday.

"Anyway, it's always been yours," he said quickly, putting those bad memories to rest. "I never wanted to give it to anyone else."

Her hands shook so hard that he had to help her open the box.

The vintage ring was lovely. A simple gold band was set with a diamond flanked by two sapphires. None of the stones was particularly large, but all three were perfect. "It's beautiful," she whispered.

Gavin closed his hand over hers. "All-in?"

She had to admit she was still a little scared. She suspected she would always worry when Gavin donned his badge and weapon and went out on the streets. Every report of an injured officer would terrify her. But she'd learn to deal with that. Maybe she'd make friends with J.T.'s wife and Avery's wife and the husbands and wives of some of Gavin's other coworkers. Maybe she'd pick up a few tips from them on how to deal with the fear. The man she loved was a cop, and he wasn't going to change until or unless he was ready for something new. Because she'd fallen in love with him—twice—just as he was, she realized she didn't even want him to change.

They'd been given a second chance. As he'd advised, she was going to appreciate every minute they had together. Starting now.

"All-in," she told him, her voice entirely steady this time.

His smile flashed in the shadows.

She set the box aside and turned to wrap herself around him, one hand sliding beneath the sheet as she pressed her mouth to his throat.

"What are you doing?" he asked, making no effort at all to resist.

She smiled up at him. "I'm enjoying the moment. Do you have a problem with that?"

She could tell by the way he hardened in her hand that he had no problems at all.

With a laugh, he flipped her onto her back and towered over her. "I could get used to this new risk-taking Jenny."

"Good," she murmured, drawing his mouth down to hers. "Because I plan to be around for a very long time."

His murmur of approval was muffled in a kiss that sealed the deal.

* * * * *

Look for Tess's story,
THE BOSS'S MARRIAGE PLAN
the next installment of Gina Wilkins's
new Special Edition miniseries
PROPOSALS & PROMISES
On sale October 2015,
wherever Harlequin books and ebooks are sold.

#2425 An Officer and a Maverick
Montana Mavericks: What Happened at the Wedding?
by Teresa Southwick

Lani Dalton needs to distract on-duty Officer Russ Campbell from her rowdy brother. Instead, they wind up locked in a cell together, where sparks ignite. Russ isn't eager to trust another woman after he had his heart stomped on once before...but the deputy might just lasso this darling Dalton for good!

#2426 The Bachelor Takes a Bride
Those Engaging Garretts!
by Brenda Harlen

Marco Palermo believes in love at first sight—now, if only he could get Jordyn Garrett to agree with him! A wager leads to a date and a sizzling kiss, but can Marco open Jordyn up to love and make her his forever?

#2427 Destined to Be a Dad
Welcome to Destiny
by Christyne Butler

Liam Murphy just discovered he's a daddy—fifteen years too late. The cowboy is taken with his daughter and her mother, Missy Dobbs. The beautiful Brit was the one who got away, but Liam knows Destiny, Wyoming, is where he and his girls are meant to be together.

#2428 A Sweetheart for the Single Dad
The Camdens of Colorado
by Victoria Pade

Tender-hearted Lindie Camden is making up for her family's misdeeds by helping out the Camdens' archrival, Sawyer Huffman, on a community project. Sawyer's good heart and even better looks soon have her dreaming of happily-ever-after with the sexy single dad...

#2429 Coming Home to a Cowboy
Family Renewal
by Sheri WhiteFeather

Horse trainer Kade Quinn heads to Montana after uncovering his long-lost son. But he remains wary of the child's mother, Bridget Wells. She once lit his body and heart on fire, and time hasn't dulled their passion for each other—and their family!

#2430 The Rancher's Surprise Son
Gold Buckle Cowboys
by Christine Wenger

Cowboy Cody Masters has only ever loved one woman—Laura, the beautiful daughter of his arrogant neighbor. So when he finds out that Laura had their child, he's shocked. Can Cody reclaim what's his and build the family he's always dreamed of with Laura and their son?

YOU CAN FIND MORE INFORMATION ON UPCOMING HARLEQUIN® TITLES, FREE EXCERPTS AND MORE AT WWW.HARLEQUIN.COM.

HSECNM0815

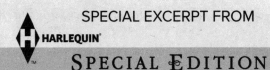
He settled his hands lightly on her hips, holding her close
but not too tight. He wanted her to know that this was
her choice while leaving her in no doubt about what he
wanted. She pressed closer to him, and the sensation of
her soft curves against his body made him ache.

He parted her lips with his tongue and she opened
willingly. She tasted warm and sweet—with a hint of
vanilla from the coffee she'd drank—and the exquisite
flavor of her spread through his blood, through his body,
like an addictive drug.

He felt something bump against his shin. Once. Twice.

The cat, he realized, in the same moment he decided
he didn't dare ignore its warning.

Not that he was afraid of Gryffindor, but he was afraid
of scaring off Jordyn. Beneath her passionate response,
he sensed a lingering wariness and uncertainty.

Slowly, reluctantly, he eased his lips from hers.

She drew in an unsteady breath, confusion swirling in her deep green eyes when she looked at him. "What… what just happened here?"

"I think we just confirmed that there's some serious chemistry between us."

She shook her head. "I'm not going to go out with you, Marco."

There was a note of something—almost like panic—in her voice that urged him to proceed cautiously. "I don't mind staying in," he said lightly.

She choked on a laugh. "I'm not going to have sex with you, either."

"Not tonight," he agreed. "I'm not *that* easy."

This time, she didn't quite manage to hold back the laugh, though sadness lingered in her eyes.

"You have a great laugh," he told her.

Her gaze dropped and her smile faded. "I haven't had much to laugh about in a while."

"Are you ever going to tell me about it?"

He braced himself for one of her flippant replies, a deliberate brush-off, and was surprised by her response.

"Maybe," she finally said. "But not tonight."

It was an acknowledgment that she would see him again, and that was enough for now.

Don't miss
THE BACHELOR TAKES A BRIDE
by Brenda Harlen,
available September 2015 wherever
Harlequin® Special Edition books and ebooks are sold.

www.Harlequin.com

Love the Harlequin book you just read?

Your opinion matters.

Review this book on your favorite book site, review site, blog or your own social media properties and share your opinion with other readers!

Be sure to connect with us at:
Harlequin.com/Newsletters
Facebook.com/HarlequinBooks
Twitter.com/HarlequinBooks

HARLEQUIN®

A *Romance* FOR EVERY MOOD™

JUST CAN'T GET ENOUGH?

Join our social communities
and talk to us online.

You will have access to the latest
news on upcoming titles and special
promotions, but most importantly,
you can talk to other fans about your
favorite Harlequin reads.

Harlequin.com/Community

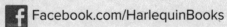 Facebook.com/HarlequinBooks

 Twitter.com/HarlequinBooks

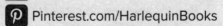 Pinterest.com/HarlequinBooks